CLARKESWORLD

D1484240

FICTI

NON-FICTION

Neil Clarke: Publisher/Editor-in-Chief
Sean Wallace: Editor
Kate Baker: Non-Fiction Editor/Podcast Director

Clarkesworld Magazine (ISSN: 1937-7843) • Issue 204 • September 2023

Stones

NNEDI OKORAFOR

I don't know if I can die. Maybe when this comet reaches the sun, I'll keep right on being. Or maybe then, finally, after so long, I will stop. I am not ready to find out. I want to be immortal. To never die as those on your planet do.

This place isn't how I remember it. It is ugly. Yet it's the place of my birth. How can that be? I have been to enough places to know what beauty is. I have not seen the entire universe, but I have seen much. To end my existence here, in the place where I started it, would negate all that I have come to believe. Of course, there is so much I will never know. Like, I don't know where I come from, or what I am.

You probably didn't expect to hear from me again. There is so much *you* could never have known, so that's understandable. But from the moment I left you, I knew I would speak to you again, and I knew it would be in this way. My mind was not light when I left you. And now I find myself a pile of stones, unable to leave this place as it hurls toward the sun, so it may be now or never. I will tell you my story, and then I will see if it's the end. I will speak in the way you and I came to communicate. It is the thing I most enjoyed during our brief time together. Knowing how to conceptualize, to define and to articulate is your second greatest gift to me.

But let me also make it clear, this message is not just me talking and telling, it is first and foremost an apology. I will say it many times in this message but let me say it this first time before I begin: I am sorry.

OK. I'm ready.

I awoke on this comet as it passed the planet of Saturn. I remember this because Saturn was the first thing I ever saw, and my very first thought was that it was lovely. I could not yet communicate it to another, but I knew what "lovely" was, I knew how to articulate it in my mind. I knew what my mind was. There was so much I understood without experience. And I instinctively knew how to bring my body together, from the tiny to large blue, gray, silver, and bronze stones. I pulled myself into the form that I would have from then on. Nebulous silver orb around my bronze head, bronze face, bronze shoulders and arms, blue body, and rocket thrusters. On the inside, I was warm, the heat I produced effortless and constant.

I don't breathe gasses as you and your kind do. I cannot imagine what it would be like to need to do such a thing. All the time. To die if I were to stop. To be unable to peruse the vacuum of space. Nevertheless, I was aware of myself. I was not part of the comet. I lifted up and hovered above its surface. I made my gray stones meld into a rocket and my silver stones tumbled and whirled around my head like the comet's long tail of stone and dust.

When I'd floated out enough to see the sun for the first time, I made my bronze face and arms shimmer in reflection of its beauty. One must honor a star. I would visit it when I was ready. For the time being, I returned to my comet and rested, watching Saturn as we moved past it. I settled into my body, turning my senses inward. What I discovered occupied me for some time. There was a universe inside me, this was the source of the heat. I gazed at it. Worlds, spaces, stones, dust, they tumbled and danced, dwelled, died, spawned. There was joy, adventure, explosion, movement, and billions of colors in me. I carried this within. Maybe it is where I come from. My *self*.

When I turned my attention outward again, I felt like more, and I saw more. The vastness of space made me want to spread and open myself to it and shout, "I am here!" I did not fear death. That is something your kind does. I was freedom. Radiation is a passing wind to me. Heat is my existence, and it comes from inside me, so I always exist.

The sun was now barely a speck. It was so cold and lonely there. I left the comet. I finally went out into the universe.

It began with a smell. The smell of planets, nebula, comets, asteroids, meteorites, dust, gases, radiation. Yes, I can actually smell them. These smells move all around me. Where they are going, I do not know. But they always tell on themselves. The smells are alive in that they tell the stories of their origins; where they came from, and how to get there. I realized this after a while. And then after a longer while, I understood that I could find the main characters of these stories the smells were telling.

The first planet I found was a planet of sulfurous gas and red ices. In finding it, I learned that I could travel through space very fast. You cannot understand what it is to travel what you consider lightyears in moments. To be human is to *not* be what I am. This is fine. But I can tell you this, it was the most enjoyable sensation I'd ever felt. I must have been made for this, to travel. In searching for and finding this first planet using the story of the smells, I came to understand my thrusters. They glowed with mighty heat and propelled me forth. The moment made my insides vibrate, and this gave me such pleasure that for a while I could do nothing but voyage, so enraptured I was in the passage of space all around me. I discovered love, for I was in love with travel.

When I reached this first planet, it gave me more joy. The fact that there was something on the end of the travel was an additional reward. This planet had an atmosphere. What a thing it was to experience for the first time. Every part of me felt a pull and then a release, like the planet was expecting, then welcoming me, then letting me explore.

I blasted toward the planet's surface, anxious to see it up close. I felt gasses in my face, against my body. On my head, what you saw as "long puffy silver hair" is just more of me. It drapes around me protectively, and when exceptionally happy and free, it spreads around my head, capturing the gasses as I fly. I spiraled and twirled toward red spikes of frozen water. I crashed through them, sending weak brittle shards all about. I screamed with laughter, slapping at the shards, dancing in the sparkles. This was the start of so much. I decided that I wanted to see everything I could see in the universe.

I had recently come into being, yes. But I already knew so much. I knew what things were, but I knew I wanted to know more. So I explored. Many many planets. Some, more than once. I burned. I froze. I vibrated. I was pressed. I was pulled. I plunged through suns. I tumbled across asteroids. I flew through the tails of comets. I visited moons. I communed with nebula. I saw much, even if it was only a fraction of what there is to see. I returned often to your solar system.

However, there was one planet I avoided. It had one of the most complex scents I'd ever smelled. A dynamic plethora of so many stories. The scent of this planet told me the strangest stories I'd ever heard. It wasn't like the others, so I stayed away from it. Eventually, though, I just wanted something different. I'd been to Jupiter, Mars, Venus, all the other planets in your solar system, I even went to the sun. I touched its surface and gave it my intense respect. In return, it gave me something, too. A tiny glowing orb of hydrogen and helium that found a home inside me, in my inner universe.

I wasn't far from your Earth when I coincidently caught its scent full on. It rushed over my senses, and I saw strange volcanoes, creatures that grew, flourished, and died, strange motion, and so much water. Hot, cool, hardened, mist. And voices. So many voices. Most planets had one voice, or three or four, always a few. This place had an uncountable number, some voices were enormous, but some were so tiny that I couldn't understand how they could be voices. And after the passage of some time, its scent had grown so much more complicated, active, and strange. Human beings, and all that human beings did, had sprung up. None of you were there the last time I had been close enough to catch Earth's scent.

My reluctant fascination and need to see this place surpassed my caution. And the great question that loomed just beneath my joy: where did I come from? It was always there with every place I traveled, the possibility of an answer to that question and the fact that it remained unanswered as I left each planet, asteroid, star, galaxy. Maybe I was from Earth. It seemed like a place that had a bit of everything. I couldn't stay away. And so, after avoiding it for so long, I flew there. If it had been your human cities and raging highways that I came across first, I'd have fled the planet immediately. However, I splashed into an ocean. Vast and blue and full of so many things. Life. I had seen water before, and I happily plunged into it, but this water was like no water I'd ever encountered in all my travels.

Wiggling, twirling, multiplying, stretching, shrinking, swimming, squishing, living, dying. Every drop had something going on in it. And there were bigger things moving about. I saw them. What you call a whale swam with me until she grew bored. For quite some time, the creature was curious. And she spoke to me, too. I could understand, just as I eventually could understand you. She asked, "What do you think?" And I said, "I don't know." But I enjoyed being with her. When she asked me if there were others, I said, "No." I had always just been "me" from the moment I was. She said no one is an "Only," and I should find them. I had nothing to say to this.

I was enjoying myself. However, not long after that, I came across my first human city. I was in the water, so it was from afar, but there were humans on the water before I reached it, too. They gave the waters a . . . twisted dense smell. I didn't like it very much. But it was the mere sight of the glowing city in the nighttime that did it. Above, I could see the stars, though the atmosphere and the lights blasting from the city drowned them out. There was noise, energy, but worst of all, way too many humans. There were more than any other large animal I'd seen since coming to this place. They overtook *everything*.

It was all too weird for me and not in a good way. And in all that weirdness, there was no one like me. I was not carbon-based, as you even told me. More than any place I'd been, Earth bothered and disappointed me most. I had no urge to greet even one human. Not long after setting my sight on that one human city, I fled the planet.

I left your solar system. For how long? In your way of measuring time? Maybe a hundred years. That is a lot for you. It is nothing for me. I sniffed out and touched many planets, large, small, hot, cold. Strange, boring. I was seeing, but I was searching, too. For someone like myself. That whale's ideas stayed with me. No one is an Only. Still, I found no one like me. Eventually, I got to thinking about my comet. I wondered if I could find it again; maybe I could find some answers on it. I knew the smell of the solar system, and soon I was close. I smelled the comet. It was near Saturn, again.

Then I saw your space station.

It was cartwheeling through space not far from Saturn. When I was last in the solar system, humans did not have that capability to go this far yet. The space station was a golden color and very shiny. It smelled bitter. I flew to it and quickly saw humans on the outside of it, tethered to the space station with cords. They were in chunky space suits, but I know what humans look like.

I stayed back and watched as they saw me and scrambled inside. This was the first time I'd allowed any human to set eyes on me. Judging by how they immediately moved toward the opening in a section of the space station, they feared me. I was amused, so I stayed and waited to see what they'd do next.

They came back out. There were ten of them. In those suits. They did not have thrusters like me, but they had something that propelled them forth. They were clumsy and unnatural here. They did not belong in space. I remember how small they were on Earth, their heads not bulbous like the helmets they wore, as I watched them from afar. Each had flesh of various shades, but none were white like these suits.

They were closer now and though they were small, I could smell them. A sweet smell that was also oily like a substance on a planet I'd once visited. They were afraid of me. Their suits gave off gasses as they approached. They were close now.

Three carried a large, long metal thing. It was a dark gray. I'm thinking of everything I have learned from you, about language, about human ways, about why why why. I did not know how I was going to communicate with these humans at the time. I wasn't thinking about that as much as I was just curious and amused. I'd visited many planets. I'd encountered other life-forms, nothing like me and nothing like those on Earth, but they were life-forms. Some I could communicate with, most I could not. None of them behaved like human beings, thankfully.

I stayed where I was as they approached. Watching them watch me. They were moving slower now, probably unsure of what I'd do. They were communicating with each other. I could hear it in waves. I waited for them to speak to me. I have learned from you, so I could have learned from them. If that had been their intent.

They pointed the long device at me, and something burst from it. It looked like blue-pink lightning. It felt like breakage. It forced me back, and they fired their weapon again, and it hit me again. And again. By the fourth time, I regained my composure . . . sort of.

I could feel the lightning rippling through every aspect of me. And not since I had come into being had I felt all that I was start fragmenting into my many stones. Instinctively, I held myself together, and when I did this . . . oh the *pain*! PAIN! I'd never *felt* pain! I knew instantly what it was, though. Still, my body exclaimed, "WHAT IS THIS!!"

The humans were already fleeing back to their space station entrance.

I don't know what happened next. I was unfamiliar with what I felt, and how I reacted. I was experiencing pain. They had caused it. I'd been waiting to greet them and instead they introduced me to a terrible sensation. In your time measurement, how old was I? Many many thousands of years. I had done nothing but explore the galaxy and feel joy and maybe even bring joy and wonder. I had harmed no one. I didn't know what harm *was*.

I pulled and held myself together. Then I reacted to the pain by lashing out. It was all I could think to do to make it stop. The cloud that floated around my head became sharp. I sliced all three of those carrying the device into pieces. Their suits opened up and their flesh separated from itself, splashing out and then freezing. I crushed their device with my stones. I moved faster than you can understand. The seven who were fleeing to the large opening in the space station had no chance. I sliced them each into pieces. I sent their parts scattering about around the space station. Some of their red liquid managed to splash across its white surface before freezing. Maybe it would eventually flake away; I didn't know.

I was in pain.

There were others inside the open entrance. I rushed into it and found myself in a large enclosure, and I could feel pressure and hear hissing as the opening behind me was suddenly cut off by a giant door. I could have just torn it open and flown off.

The pain I was in made me angry. I had never felt anger before. I glared into the opening in front of me. I could see more humans. Staring back at me. This was them with no suits. Whatever they had done to me was still happening, and I had to make an effort to keep myself together. What had been easy was now so difficult, and this fueled my anger even more.

I tore open their door. Your air, the pressure, even the hint of weight I felt did nothing to me. I have been to many planets. Each of them has a smell and a feel. I always adjust. It was no different here, even while fighting to stay together. There was sound here, from the humans, from their vehicles. They fled like the creatures I saw on Earth. They did not have another weapon to shoot at me, not one that made any difference. Where they were small, I was much bigger. I could not fit easily into their space. But because I was falling apart, I could squeeze in, changing the shape of my body.

When you saw me, you described me as "a giant human robot monster." You said I was shiny and that when I moved, I crushed everything around me. You saw me after I'd managed to pull myself together, just before I could do it no more. What must these people have seen? A wide enormous shiny metal face and silver cloud filling their walkways? My thrusters were behind me, incinerating the walls and equipment as I tore through the space station.

I wreaked havoc. I killed several humans. I left a trail of mutilated bodies and blood. I could smell each of you, so no one was safe. I was angry. I was in pain. And then I found myself in front of your door.

I looked inside and came face-to-face with you. I clutched the doors to rip them open. I had killed every human on board but you. Your head would come off as easily as all the others, your insides would spill out like Earth's waters. The smells of metal and dirt would rise from your quivering flesh as you fell. But in that moment, instead, I paused. I do not know human beings, so I could not read the look on your face. I didn't even understand the arrangement of your face. But you stood there. You did not flee or start making noise or try to shoot a weapon at me. That gave me pause.

And then I fell apart. I simply couldn't hold myself together anymore. Into a heap of stones. I lay there for some time. Then you finally decided to come out. I remember the sound of the doors opening because it sounded like four doors had to open for you to come out. I could still smell things, too. The gas that plumed out when you emerged smelled like some of the places on Earth. Where the green and brown creatures who grew in the dirt lived.

You cowered for a while before you came and stood over me. You kicked one of my stones, and I tried with all my might to pull myself together, but I could not. I only caused a ripple of lightning to roll over me. You jumped back but did not flee. You had a device in your hands. You ran off and were gone for some time. When you returned, you were breathing heavily.

You stood over me for a long time. Then you touched one of my stones. Picked it up. Examined it. You said something to me, and I was surprised when I understood it. "Listen," you said. Then you began to gather up my stones. At this point, I could not even attempt to pull myself together. Whatever they had shot me with had taken all that.

One by one, you brought my stones into those doors, to a very strange place. It was full of that smell. You spoke as you moved me. And I understood what you said. You told me that you'd studied a comet that was now on a collision course with the sun as it passed Saturn, and my stones looked to be made of the same material. You said you suspected this because you'd studied materials you'd mined from that comet for many years. You knew it when you saw it. You said that maybe I was born of that comet. I wanted to say more, but I couldn't speak. I could only listen.

When you brought the stones that were my head to the room you were piling them in, I saw that you actually weren't alone. More of those creatures that lived in the dirt that I had seen on Earth were here. But a different type. They grew on the walls in the large room and hung down, winding themselves into a large, coiling bundle that quivered and hummed. They were purple and reminded me of nebula that I had flown through in my journeys.

I had killed everyone on your space station. They did something to me, and I could not help myself. I was in pain. I was angry. I had memories of your planet that were bad. Humans had done something to me that was bad.

However, still, I send you this message to tell you I am sorry. This was not like me. I do not know where I am from. You say I came from this comet that is now heading into the sun. Maybe this is true. But I am not one who extinguishes life, kills things alive. I am an explorer, a seer, a traveler, one who journeys to witness the universe. So I am sorry, Listen Chukwuma. I speak your name because you taught me how to. Your name itself is an incantation. You are named Listen, and I listened.

How well, did I listen? I can recite all that you told me as, instead of killing me, you healed me.

Unlike the others, you spoke to me from the beginning. And I quickly began to understand. As you spoke, you poured water on me.

Then some other things. I remember your words like a prayer to the sun. You said:

Listen to me. Call me Listen Chukwuma because that is my name. I don't know what you are. I think that you are female. Even if you are a pile of rocks. I saw you from my console when you first appeared. I told the others that they should be kind to you, but they were afraid. We have been on this space station, that is what this place is, for fifteen years. All of us have become strange.

However, you appeared. A thirty-foot-tall woman-creature spaceship in space. Menacing with that halo of silver hair that floated all around you. Eyes that flashed like storms on Jupiter. A giant thruster that could scorch our entire space station. All people saw was a threat. Like some kind of Godzilla thing. On Earth Godzilla is a kaiju, a great beast who makes no sense to anyone. Could you blame them? Some of the engineers had been working on a machine that could cause molecules to disassemble. We do not have guns here. So they used that on you. It's all they could think of.

They were yelling at each other when you first appeared. I was at the meeting. Attending virtually, as always. Through the cam. Everyone was shouting. They were afraid. They saw a monster, an alien. We are not even on Earth, and they saw an "alien"; we are the aliens out here. Strike first they decided. I tried yelling, too. "Wait," I said. "Try and see!" But no one could hear me. Everyone was on their feet, yelling, someone even knocked over the robot that housed my camera. It was still on the floor when everyone left.

Let me explain, I have not left my lab in ten years. To help you, I stepped through those doors for the first time since I began here. I was not confined to my lab out of fear or because I was a prisoner. My confinement was my choice. Now I am alone here until others come. But that is an issue for later.

I am from Owerri. I come from a family of farmers. One of the last in my country to actually farm yam. Most of the country's land is now dedicated to growing periwinkle grass and all the other produce farms are owned and operated by Ultimate Corp. I was expected to follow in my parents' footsteps. As my three sisters and two brothers did. My family is wealthy. Independent. I was the youngest. Like everyone in my family, I loved the dirt, the soil, it is in my blood. But I wanted to study the dirt and soil on other planets, comets, the rocks hurling through space. I became a geologist, and then an astronaut.

Fifteen years ago, I was sent on a mission to explore debris collected from Saturn's rings and really anything else we found. At the end of those two years, I found more than rocks and dust in my research. One day I saw something shimmering as it slowly floated by. I went out in my suit to collect some of it. When I brought it to my lab, I found that it was exactly what I thought it was: spores.

When I presented my finding to the space station team, everyone was fascinated. When I said I wanted to nourish the spores and see what they grew into, everyone was up in arms. I asked them what I was even here for if not this. Extraterrestrial seed! I had been studying for exactly this all my life. When I spoke to my sisters and brothers back home, they crowded around the camera to tell me what I already wanted to do: make it grow, they shouted.

I made a deal with everyone on the space station and our governments on Earth. I would cultivate the spores in this lab. It has its own air circulation, water source, food was delivered by robots. My family was behind me all the way. We are people who grow plants. And so here I am. One decade. And you see that I have succeeded. I do not know what these plants are, but I know they can receive and send messages using radio waves. Through their leaves, I have heard things from across the galaxy, maybe even universe. I don't know how much you will understand if I explain it to you. I don't quite have the vocabulary for it yet. Someday, I will. And I have seen no one in person for ten years. And now, you have killed everyone on this space station. I am seven years away from Earth.

All this you told me as you nourished me. Stabilized me. Revived me. How did you know how to treat me? To bring me back? To reverse whatever it was that the device did? As you worked, I came to master your form of communication. Now I knew your story.

"Why?" was the first thing I said to you.

"Because it is what I am," you said.

You immediately began to take my stones one by one to another place, the large space I'd come through where the doors had closed behind me. The doors were still shut, everything in the room cleared.

"What are you," you asked as you moved my stones.

"I am me."

"You don't know?"

"What else is there to know?"

"Why did you come here?"

"I have been to your planet; I have seen humans before. I was afraid then. But this time I was curious."

"You should not have come."

"I know that now."

"When I first saw you arrive, I thought you were some sort of spirit," you said.

I said nothing to this.

"If I cure you . . . do you know what that is? Cure?"

"Yes."

"If I cure you, will you kill me?"

"No."

You left me then. All my stones in that room. I wanted to ask you what you would do now. Would others come? Were you able to be alone as I was? You knew where you were from, what you were. And it seemed humans were always with other humans. Even out there in space. At that time, I did not care to apologize. I was still angry. What the other humans had done to me was wrong and cruel and unearned.

You'd left something beside my stones. A device. After you left, it buzzed and sparked and one of those sparks jumped and popped onto the nearest of my stones. And within moments, I ignited with electricity. Then I was up. The doors opened, revealing broken doors; these were the ones I had ripped open. I flew out. I only looked back when the space station was but a speck in the distance. I went on to visit Jupiter a fourth time. But when I left it, I was in pain again.

Listen Chukwuma, you brought me back, but you did not cure me.

I did not want to fall apart in space, so I sniffed out the nearest solid place. It was as if it were meant to be because that place turned out to be the comet you told me about. The comet I'd been looking for when I was distracted by your space station. The comet that was also my place of origin. I had not seen it in so long. I landed on its surface and immediately let myself disintegrate into a pile of stones again. This comet was my place of origin, would it be my place of end? My chariot into death? *Would* I die? *Could* I die?

So here I am. A pile of stones again. On the comet hurling toward the sun. Will you get this message through your mysterious plant friend? I don't know. I can send radio waves and receive them. I could hear your plant speaking while you healed me. I asked it what it was, and it told me more than I will ever know about myself, I suspect. It had an entire history, and it was so proud. You were part of its history. So I suspect you will get this message. If you are alive. I hope you are alive.

Listen, I am sorry. I am sorry for killing all those humans. I am sorry for leaving you there all alone. Fully alone. For years. Who knows the damage I did to your home. You were doing your life's work with those alien plants. I can tell you what they were, for I have seen them on a distant planet. And what you grew was never so healthy and lush on their home moon. You are a good farmer. Your family should be proud, Listen.

Send.

She was nothing but stones on a comet. She could look around, but she could not collect herself and fly away. For over a millennia, she'd traveled the galaxy. There was so much more to see, but she would never do that. She was sure of it. The sun was close now and parts of the comet were beginning to melt and sizzle, its tail growing longer than ever. She still did not know where she came from or if there were others like her, but she would have to be fine with that.

A year later, she flew with the comet into the sun and that was that.

. . . Except it wasn't. It took her three years to emerge from the other side of the sun, and when she did, she was not on the comet. Her comet was gone. Burned up before it even reached the sun's corona. And there were two things she knew for certain, the first the sun had taught her, and the second Listen had taught her. What the sun taught her was that she could not die. Why she'd ever thought she could was laughable now. She was not like the creatures on Earth, never had been.

The second thing that she now knew after traveling through the sun, she acted on immediately. She shot off, sniffing and sniffing. For her, it was not long, only a few hundred years. She found the comet with multiple nuclei far beyond the solar system. Far from the strange planet called Earth. The comet was heading in a direction she was curious about, and she decided to stay on it for a while. As she knew she would, on its several surfaces, she found more stones. In time, those stones gathered and became.

There was no name for what she was, but there were more like her on this large comet. Five of them. She taught them everything she knew and soon, they left the comet, a powerful and bonded family of travelers. And they saw much. And continue to do so to this day. Because the universe is full of infinite wonders.

ABOUT THE AUTHOR

Nnedi Okorafor is a *New York Times* Bestselling writer of science fiction and fantasy for both children and adults. She is the winner of Nebula, World Fantasy, Eisner, Lodestar, Locus Award and multiple Hugo Awards and her debut novel *Zahrah the Windseeker* won the prestigious Wole Soyinka Prize for Literature. Nnedi has also written comics for Marvel, including *Black Panther: Long Live the King, Wakanda Forever* (featuring the Dora Milaje), and the *Shuri* series. Nnedi has several works in development for TV and film. She lives with her daughter Anyaugo in Phoenix, AZ.

The Queen of Calligraphic Susurrations

D.A. XIAOLIN SPIRES

Winli plucked off one of the remote-controlled bees and placed him back into the crystalline hive. It was a beautiful thing, with workers visible like an ant farm. Far from the sliced partitions of beekeeping past that sat in a rectangular box, these new see-through hives mimicked a natural formation of an organic hive, lumpy and looking something like a rounder pineapple.

Beekeeping was her inherited occupation, but her love was writing.

Unfortunately, the bees equipped with exoskels and interactive helmets kept her busy enough that all the workshops scrawled in digital sumi on the weekends of her holocal would vanish. With a swipe of her hand, she would send these anticipated events to the compost bin. She didn't have the time. Or maybe it was the fortitude. Though, possessing a lack of resolve wasn't something she was going to admit to herself. She shook her wrist a few times and let it hang. Her fingers ached. With her holobrush in one hand, she held her sleeve back with the other. She lifted her elbow, swiped a few words in the air with her still-throbbing wrist, and immediately hit "wipe away." Sometimes she tried aerokeying, tapping in invisible artifacts in the air instead of the texture-rich affair of generating strokes in her own penmanship with a holobrush. It never sounded . . . right. After her Sisyphean act of committing to two hundred stylized characters that would immediately disappear by her own hand, she gave up and tended to the bees. At least she did not condemn them to nothingness with a swipe of her index finger, like she did with her script. The bees were active, alive, making delicious golden treacle-like treasure. At least something was making something valuable in this home, she mumbled. The bees followed instinctive cues, working autonomously most of the time, but with some remote guidance on her end to maximize quantity production. If only she could be so fruitful.

"A Story about Beekeeping" was the title of her story. She frowned. *It's not very creative.* She tapped at her teeth with her nails, making an intermittent clinking sound. Her fingers had the digital ghostscape of sumi ink on her fingers. This splash of black ink would disappear once she closed the Implementation. She was hoping that a creative writing course would teach her how to be creative. But she never got there. *There's never enough time,* she thought, flexing her neck, her lips turned downward. At the corner of her holoscroll was an earmarked Vision she kept inactive. It drew to her, pulling her gaze toward her periphery. It was an ad, a trial offer to test out an AI writer. She tried to drive the thought away, but like the buzzing in her ears from the energetic bees, the energetic calisthenics of an anthropomorphized ink brush distracted her. It jumped up and down, marking that Vision space with splashes of tiny sumi ink dots that would fade away in seconds. The traces of those little dots, that brush activity, burned in Winli's eyes. She wanted her story to have that verve, that immediacy and urgency that her stilted writing style simply could not, would not convey, no matter how many voxels of time she stole away, allocating them to her covert passion.

She closed her eyes tight, bit her teeth together hard, and said, "Ah, starlight and sweet cybernated sucker. I'm going to have to do it." She pitched the generated inkstone behind her, and it left a ghostly streak of ink that faded and twinkled away. Winli gestured to the top right, where the ad barely peeked from view, and picked up the brush. It had a heady smell, like artificial ink, that veered too much on the mothball side of the aroma equation than the more earthy whiffs of analog sumi ink. *They really put some cash into this Implementation,* she thought. Adding holoscents to a program was above and beyond. She cringed, the calculations of company expenditures and passing costs to users summing up in her head. This was going to be expensive. Once her fingers grasped over the bouncing brush, her wrist tensed. The start of a headache pounded in her temples, and she winced. The meaning of an apparitional tone shot through her and went unvoiced but understood. *Does she accept the one hundred eighty creds to take on the dynabrush?* The thought bounced up and down in her mind and would not leave her, even when she loosened her grip. The whiff of mothballs strengthened, a kind of professional-grade cleaner heady in her nostrils. The buzz in her ears got louder, but it was a phantom sound, one she imagined since she knew that her bees in their crystalline hive could not be that loud through the patent material. Her mouth whispered *no, no*, but her mind had said *yes*. It flashed with a splash that would be digitally recorded, a splice of neural imagery that would confirm that she did in fact agree. This record would be sealed into the Implementation's archives, corroborating assent.

Suddenly, on her arm, from her fingers up to her elbow, wispy dots appeared, like bunny footprints in snow. It was the intro dance of the dynabrush, the pounding in her temples told her, assessing her physiological state, so it could mimic some of the expression that she might bring to life. The program bore into her bloodstream, into her red blood cells, and delved deep into her anatomical self to pull out something it called the idiosyncratic articulation of words unique to each individual presence. She felt something worm its way up and down her body and then through her sinuses and into her brain. It felt impossibly odd, a wiggly zap, something that should not be. On the Vision, it scrawled out a body, with the appropriate curves and muscles in seconds and filled it with sensory notes, like a wine taster judging the body, aroma, appearance, and finish of a glass of a particularly impeccable vintage specimen. The scroll turned and a new space appeared, a blinking light. A flash in between her temples acknowledged that she understood the question. *What is your prompt?*

Her left hand quivered, partly out of nerves, and partly out of holding such an electrifying dynabrush that did not seem to ever simply be inanimate. Instead, it hummed and buzzed and jumped and little feathery black dots appeared in her vision, like gnats splatting against the cornea of a runner sprinting through a trail of dense trees. She blinked moisture, her eyelashes wet, her vision cloudy, trying to get the dots out. She couldn't. They were a part of the program, a distinctive specter of the Implementation. And she was one hundred and eighty creds poorer for it. How many hours would that be tending to the bees? How much of their rich superhoney would she have to sell to the Institute to cover that? She did not want to think, did not want to do the math. *Just go with it.* She already had consented, she was bound to the agreement. *Okay,* she whispered to herself. Her lips trembled. *Here it goes.*

"A story about beekeeping." "Drone warfare." "Love between different bee factions." She added a bit of flavor after each input, sometimes strengthening some of the imagery and detailing with flairs and finesse. She had longed to elaborate on that pun, on drones, the male bees variety and the flying machinery variety, delving into and playing on that connection. She started to grin, becoming slightly delirious with the power of the dynabrush, her knuckles turning white. The dark dots continued to materialize on her skin, appearing as even more of a contrast against her arms. They were draining color moment by moment, as if the program were sucking out her innards, her blood, her life force. It was not, she knew. It was just the imagery created by the program loading, a kind of phantasmic theater to project an image of commingling, her own self and the AI combining, producing something together. A symphonic blend, a dance of fusion. Interflowing elixirs of truth and fantasy creating a potion of a magically compelling narrative. It was a ploy of the program to make it feel more alive and fantastical than it actually was. And it worked.

The brush was bounding so hard, she gripped her right hand on top of her left, trying to will the brush in place enough to not feel as if everything was spiraling out of control. She felt like it was though, going out of control, no matter how much she tried to reign it in. Her heart rate accelerated, and a jolt went through her spine. Her chest ached, and for a moment, it must be a figment of her imagination she never thought was so active, but it looked as if her belly had been distended. Like something would pop out of her at any minute. Tiny dots filled her eyes, and they looked to have populated her stomach as well, or maybe they were a projection of her eyes. She knew it was all a projection, just a part of the program, the holo's Implementation that made it feel so alive and real.

An ecstatic burst convulsed through her, and she screamed. Bees buzzed louder. Wings, thousands of wings, twisting and rotating, transparent and glittering came into her blotched view. They were blurry, but she had the faint impression they had tiny headbands, as if remotely controlled like the analog helmet-wearing workers she manipulated for pay. These digital creatures shrunk, their wings diaphanous, with light trickling through. They became so small, little glints of jewels. They arranged themselves into strokes, pollinating through the Vision as if it were a wildflower field on a windless sunny day, zigzagging in wingbeat susurruses.

A taste of sickly honey filled her mouth. It was too rich, too sweet, like calsyrup, used on the otherwise flavorless chalky helonbars, faux egg crepes, and limp flomein noodles. It made her gag, and she coughed. Static ink came flying out of her mouth and stuck to the Vision, arranging itself into more characters, covering the infinitesimal bees, filling in the crevices between other words, which edged out to make room for them. The brush sank deeper into her hand, as if compelling her fingers to grip it tighter and tighter. Her knuckles popped, and she took in an involuntary breath, her whole torso sinking in so that her rib cage stuck out, the distended stomach turned inward. Her vision went blurry.

She released the breath, the whole breadth of the canvas of words appearing before her again. She grimaced. It was a pretty visceral way to create a story, harrowing even, but she supposed it was more synergistic than the older models of AI that just took her words and ran with it. This version involved her whole self, from head to toe, and fused it with the movements of the ink to create calligraphic concinnity.

She told herself to later look through the terms of agreement—that nobody ever looks through—before swiping yes to see if the agreement said anything about these brutal contortions of her body. She told herself that she must, she would do it later, but she knew, though, that she really wouldn't. Nobody reads those things. They're just legal decoration, a sprinkling of respecting this and that right and no deception and fraudulent blah blah character salad. With certain Visions, at the terms of agreement progression, something snazzy occurs. She recalled launching a program only to be confronted with an animated character appearing in ethereal light rapping out the words to an upbeat syncopation. It did not at all compel her to listen. It compelled her to mute the character, she thought wryly. She didn't know what user would actually entertain listening to that violation of a perfectly excellent genre of music, given the lethal combination of accelerated garble and insipidness. She'd rather spend a full day recalibrating the remote helmets. It seemed more fun to tackle adjusting sensors located in individual hive cells for optimization than combing through that bland and stilted language.

She was recovering from the onslaught of the ink storm, shivering, cold now all over. The black dots were fading to gray, and her teeth chattered. Before her, the Vision space was covered in text that was shifting in size. The rather large characters squeezed and squeezed into a smaller size to fit all of them onto one Vision space, like commuters making themselves narrow to fit on benches in the elevated autodrive bus trails. Her eyes were still blurry, and her head throbbed, but she could make out some of the writing. She read, twirling the now loosened dynabrush in her strained fingers. The text told a story about a robot worker drone, all filamental antenna and wire wings, at an enormous bee factory coming to sentience and wreaking havoc on vertically grown crops. It was sending messages through crop spheres, as creepy as crop circles but in 3D, in a clandestine code. When it was read, it spread like a virus, activating other robot drone worker bees. They amassed into a mechanical military and armed themselves with a synthetic tar. The synthetic tar they distilled from honey and other artificial sweeteners to take on the oppressors who have too long repressed and exploited their colonies. It was fantastic, she surmised. The narrative had heroism, symbology, and acted as a kind of parable. It was so good, it could even become a staple, something in classroom curricula, she bemused. She had forgotten about being cold. She had even held her breath at some parts and cried at the end. It was that good. The cold came back to her after the second reread. When she was done, she shook, letting out an emotional cathartic gasp. That was when it hit her. *This was it.* This was the writer she was always meant to be. The writer that she had become—through the dynabrush, still clasped so tightly in her hands. She quickly made duplicate versions of the narrative, paying with a clink of creds for each copy that she saved into her Archive, and dropped the brush, staring at her strangely sick-looking flesh. *She did this?* she thought. She could still see the fading of the dots, shrinking and tiny. There were so many they were uncountable.

She licked her lips, clapped her hands, and pulled out a copy from her Archive. She made a few typographic adjustments and took an electronic chisel to modify the formatting here and there. Once satisfied, she sent it off, the holoscroll leaving a graphic of a part of the silk scroll being cut off with shears, folded into a dragon boat that rowed away of its own accord to the appointed destination. Its wake left a golden wave that sprayed her with an electric foam. She smiled, shaking out her hair, which was dry but felt strangely damp. Her body felt like itself again, limber and agile, rather than the taut, scrunched, tense thing it had momentarily transformed into during the process of manuscript creation. She felt like a slack small-siyah, a horn archery bowstring released, all the stress dissolved into an eerie elation. She felt a warmth flow through her, one that was raw with a pleasant heat. If she could imagine how a usurpation swarm must feel defeating a queen-right colony that had outnumbered them, that must have been what it was like. A sense of glory, of relief and confident expectation. How could she feel differently? One of her life goals was on its way to possible fulfillment.

For weeks, she waited, mostly tinkering with these bees and their exoskels. She brewed concoctions with their souped-up honeys, trying to find ways to make them more calorie dense and playing with the floral scent of their output and the blooms of taste when consumed. Of course, she was in anticipation—waiting, waiting—but she knew to be patient. She knew she could wield the dynabrush again and start the process over. But, the act of creation had siphoned so much of her, both physically, mentally, and monetarily. It was an expensive price to pay, and she had to make up for it. Besides, she was preoccupied, whether she wanted to be or not. The bees were so busy, flitting to and fro, fulfilling commands, made by their queen—as well as the Queen behind the curtain. The surreptitious human one that pulled their figurative strings.

She was using a laser to cut through the outer layer of a tiny helmet, smaller than a pinky nail clipping, to fix the severed circuits within when she heard a rapid flapping of a thousand buzzing bees, an onslaught of a wave of ventilation through the wings. It wasn't her bees making the noise. It was a sound she had produced through an audio program, crafted specifically to append to the delivery program. The sound signified receipt of a message from a sender who she had marked as of utmost importance.

The message was in a holo 摺紙 zhezhi, a part of the holoscroll that visually displayed higher dimensions folded into lesser ones, which unraveled before the recipient. Well-known senders, elite literary sites, and businesses would hire specialty topological designers to create these fantastical foldings that still had a whiff of the historical zhezhi traditions from which they drew. It was a kind of signature stamp, but they varied greatly depending on the message and recipient, like works of an artist with a canon of recognizable paintings.

Her heart pounded. The excitement in her shot forth in magnitudes, and she wrung her hands remembering the feeling of the dynabrush in her hand, and how it squeezed and squeezed. Her tongue felt similarly squeezed, her lips dry. In the middle of the folded world was a pagoda, constructed of a fine weave of silk scroll, rendered into an exquisite holo, incredibly dainty and delicate, as gossamer as bees' wings.

She stepped in, her being sublimating into an avatar that walked right in. The pagoda turned a crimson red, twirled, and shone, and she two-stepped a jig in delight, thinking, this must be it. This is the answer she was waiting for.

Scrolls unraveled from each face of the first floor of the five-storied pavilion, one at a time. She rushed to read them, starting from the one that unraveled first. Her footsteps in the holo were light and rang with bells that jangled at her ankle. She felt like a usurping wild queen bee again, but this time with no absconding swarm in tow. She was alone here, in this sanctified space. The wind whistled through the panels, rippling through the scrolls. It sounded quite realistic, and the chill that made her body shudder was no less laced with frigid authenticity.

The sky turned dark. A rain began to patter on the pagoda roofs in an ominous rhythmic beat.

A storm. It was not a good sign. Like natural disasters of dynasties past that signified emperor incompetence. A menacing flash of lightning lit up the skies and faded as she sheltered in the pagoda.

Her excitement waned. A spasm went down her back.

No, no, she murmured.

The blotches of ink shifted, like a gust through a paddy of hegemonic rice stalks. They got wet, blurred, and rearranged themselves.

She read, shaking her head.

Thank you for your submission. We were intrigued by your story but noted a peculiarity in your submission. Through extensive forensics, we were able to come to the conclusion that the manuscript was not authored solely by the named author(s) but also by artificial means, generated through a complex paid algorithm. Unfortunately, we are not accepting artificially generated text at this time. Please clearly read through the instructions before submission. We appreciate your interest and please feel free to submit original work produced by sentient legal-person(s) author(s) for consideration.

Winli's body went cold, and her fingers ached, suddenly disabused of her fanciful ideas of winning one of the top prizes, the trophy in her hands evanescing. *But, but,* her mind protested. The view before her—of the storm, flapping wet scrolls, and raised ceiling—started to fade. She grasped at the scrolls, walked over to the pagoda columns, and tried to stretch her arms over them. *No, wait*, she cried.

That clenching sense of the dynabrush gripped her fist, and she pounded at the column, as its brilliant crimson turned gray. *No!* Dots filled her eyes as anguish overcame her. How could this be the assessment? It was her body, her senses, her innards. Her physiological landscape the dynabrush had siphoned up and regurgitated. How could it not be a creation of her own being? Sure, she used the medium of technology, but one could say the same of holobrushes and aerokeys. They converted her strokes into characters on the Vision. Why should dynabrush be treated any differently?

She shrieked the sound of despair, one of an antipredator pipe in a hive, an acoustic alarm raised at attacking hornets by petrified bees. No, no, this can't be. The flavor of impending success turned bitter in her lips, honey turning to over-steeped tea leaves, moldy and acrid.

She fumbled for the exit, tripping, the bells on her ankles ringing, the tinkling turned shrill like a siren. She escaped and rushed. She would not take it. She could not.

Rejection was not a possibility.

She immediately pulled the Implementation out, the trial offer expired. Without a thought, she paid the exorbitant amount for a subscription. *Starlight and sweet cybernated sucker*, she said, with conviction. *I will write it.*

The dynabrush in her came to life, and she turned leopard-like, the ink splotch spots on her darkening, thickening, like tar, dripping like lava. With the lava ink that burned through the holoscroll in an acrid tang, she wrote. Was it the AI or was it her? She did not know. It bore through her being, making her back arch, her torso cave in, her thighs protrude, her cheeks billow. All skin and joints splattered with ink flecks. With the mighty implement in her stiff hand, she wrote and wrote. The drone army became cavalry now, bees riding on robotic flying steeds. In fact, she wrote sentience into their beings, took away prompts from a higher commander. No, there was no need for commands; no need for an outside authority to dictate the cues. They knew their places and would voice their own mandates. With authority vested in these creatures, they raced through oppressor fields, obliterating their foes. Honey, or, rather, something dark and sweet, like molasses, filled her nose. Ink sizzled and took out the naysayers, wiped them clean through. Her story filled with words like rampage, frenzy, and destruction, guided by immensely gruesome viscosity, a mucilaginous smoldering, a deluge of heat. Its rage melted through the words, through the holoscroll, through the Vision itself, until she felt completely tickled by electric sumi, exonerated from the shackles of copyright, authenticity, and legitimacy, and exiled into a space where none of it mattered, nothing but frenetic and swarmingly passionate warfare. Around her came the sound of innumerable flapping wings, righteous and unstoppable.

ABOUT THE AUTHOR

D.A. Xiaolin Spires steps into portals and reappears in sites such as Hawai'i, NY, various parts of Asia and elsewhere, with her keyboard appendage attached. Her work appears in publications such as *Clarkesworld, Analog, Nature, Terraform, Fireside, Star*Line, Liquid Imagination,* and anthologies such as *Make Shift, Ride the Star Wind, Sharp and Sugar Tooth, Deep Signal,* and *Battling in All Her Finery.* Select stories can be read in German, Spanish, Vietnamese, Estonian, French and Japanese translation.

A Guide to Matchmaking on Station 9

NIKA MURPHY

The number one thing to remember about matchmaking on Station 9 is to keep your hyper-synesthesia under control. When the client sitting across from you huffs and purses her lips, and trails of gray and beige puffs follow her every move, under no circumstances should you tell her she will never find a bashert with that kind of aura.

"Is this it?" Naomi says, swiping to the last page of the potential matches you've hand-selected for her. The outer edges of her words curdle in your stomach.

"I'm afraid you've exhausted your options," you say. Do not hold your breath even though whatever she says reeks of sour milk.

"That's disappointing. I was told you were the best shadchan this side of the asteroid belt." Her hand grazes your fingers when she hands back the list. Her skin emits a brass sections' worth of cacophony.

Do not curse your telepathy in moments like these. Remember, here, on Station 9, it is an asset. Be thankful you are no longer considered a nuisance or marked as a threat. Be thankful you no longer have to hide who you are from your family, your friends, your lover.

Naomi is half your age, but her eyes are as heavy with grief as yours. You want to tell her she is searching for the wrong partner. She needs someone able to withstand the weight of her crushed heart. Do not tell her this. Tell her you will try again.

You have no choice. You need the money. You've almost saved enough to pay off your asylum contract. Almost. Just a few more shidduchim, and you're on the first ship to Station Zero where your daughter and newborn granddaughter await your arrival.

When Naomi leaves, you scroll through your contacts until you reach Leeya's number. You type a message. Your thumb lingers for a moment.

Before you press send, ask yourself, are you really that desperate? Is there really no one else who can help you? Have you checked your database for all eligible suitors throughout Stations 9 and 10? Have you exhausted all your other resources? Isn't there anyone else on Station 11 you can call?

You know there isn't. You've made sure of that with your strategic alliances and mergers and acquisitions. You've fought and clawed your way to the top. And now, you're alone.

"Free for a consult?" your message reads.

Eight seconds later, Leeya responds with, "I'm busy."

"You owe me," you say.

Eight more minutes go by before she sends you a time and location on 10.

"See you soon," you say.

Three dots blink at the bottom of your conversation, then disappear.

Spaceflight requires an excess of willpower. Try not to feel like a canned sardine, no matter how much the odor reminds you of one. Carry a vial of frankincense oil for such occasions. Dab it on your mask. Relax. Push Leeya's face out of your mind.

An hour passes before the drumroll of three hundred passengers' chatter fades into the hum of the engines. Their dreams are impenetrable to you, thank g-d. Close your eyes and fall asleep. For once, your dreams are free of Leeya.

The flight attendant wakes you for breakfast. She is blissfully empty-headed save for the menu. The meal options swirl about her like stars around a knocked-out cartoon character. Something about her mouth reminds you of—

"None for me, thank you," you say, snipping off the end of that thought. Do not think of Leeya again until you dock.

When you finally emerge from the spaceport, you slip into familiar scents like an old pair of shoes. Ocean spray and baked sand and fried batter.

In the baggage area, an android flashes your name across their chest display. Wrap your scarf around your head so they don't spot you. You're the one in control. Not her. Don't let her dictate your arrival.

"I sent an andy for you," Leeya texts.

Wait until the train leaves the spaceport before you respond.

"Must have missed them."

Silence your messages for the rest of the ride. Enjoy the scenery. After all, Station 10 is the only other location you are allowed to travel to. The streets bustle with androids mingling among people in the last refuge for discontinued machines. They're not allowed to travel anywhere either, else they face decommissioning. Such is the price of their asylum. At least you'll be able to leave one day. Remember this as you prepare to meet Leeya.

Smooth your skirt as you wait in front of the restaurant overhanging the station's edge. Ignore the urge to smoke. It's been four decades since your last cigarette.

Your pulse quickens when Leeya's silhouette appears in the distance. As she nears, it beats loud enough to break glass.

She stands before you. Your eyes snap to hers, her clothes, her hair, her gloves. Black on black on black. Every sense in your body tunes to her frequency. She is framed in violet flames.

"Esme, so good to see you," she says and leans in to touch your cheek to hers in Station 11 fashion. Be careful not to faint from her fragrance. Lilac on the surface, milled soap beneath. It morphs into a waltz in your mind, one you've danced a thousand times, and teleports you to the past. To late nights in your shared flat on Earth, making love, compiling biodata spreadsheets. To early morning screaming matches and midday make up sex. To the moment you could no longer stand to be in the same room.

Her thoughts were clear as rain when you told her you wanted to end the relationship. She wished you well. Made not one move to change your mind. She'd known what she was going to do by then. Perhaps, she'd already done it.

Try not to speculate. Remember your goal.

She orders for you. You choose the wine.

"I have an especially difficult client who has declined or rejected every potential partner in my database," you begin, right down to business. "If I share her details with you, would you be willing to comb your database for a match? We can split the fee." You pass her Naomi's profile.

She clips a pair of reading glasses on her nose. Always the bio-purist. You had your presbyopia correction surgery years ago.

"She's unreasonable," Leeya says.

Turn your focus to the gravity-farmed microgreens, to the myriad stars in the two hundred and seventy-degree view. You may not hear her thoughts the way you hear the waitstaff gossiping in the corner, but Leeya's voice tastes like buttercream and champagne, and from that you deduce she wants something from you.

"Is there something else?" you ask, trying to keep the anger from peppering your voice.

"You seem tired. Have you considered retirement?" Leeya says this as she peers at you over her glasses, and her words crystallize into sugar. "Let's make a bet. If I can find your picky princess a match, you sell me your business at a discount."

"It's not enough you took my life and daughter away from me? You want my business too?" Don't tell her you were planning to sell it anyway. She wants to control you.

"You're still angry about that? It's been two decades," she says with fishhooks between each word. Distance and time have done nothing to quell her hatred for you. This is all she has left. Get through this, and you never have to see her ever again.

"Alright, it's a deal. But if you don't deliver, you pay off my asylum contract."

She smiles, claps, and calls the server over to settle the bill. "On me," she says, then offers you a ride. Decline.

It's been a while since you've been to Station 10. The air here is warm and welcomes a walk. Stop in front of an art gallery. Admire the watercolors in the window. An older woman sidles up next to you.

"I just love the colors in that one, don't you?" she says.

"Yes, they remind me of being in love, once," you say.

"I wish I could remember that feeling."

Go ahead and examine her. Wrinkles carve rivers over her widowed face. Still, she radiates pinks and yellows, and when you tune into her, it is like having your face cradled in her mittened hands.

"Would you like to? Remember the feeling?"

"I'm flattered, but I'm afraid I'm straighter than an android on a bicycle lane." She blushes, not unembarrassed, and you tell her the embarrassment is all yours.

"I'm a professional matchmaker," you say and tell her to call you when she's ready to find love.

"Maybe the universe has brought us together," she says.

"She is a master matchmaker, that one," you say.

Leeya meets you at a café in Midstation. She sets an espresso cup next to a tablet.

"Are those potential matches?"

She smiles, and though you resist, you dial into her anyway. The smallest details give her away now. The curves of her fingernails. The dimple in her bottom lip. The way her earlobe sags from years of wearing heavy earrings. Each feature, each blink, each breath paints sensory murals around her. Orange denials. A pluck of the harp for every dollar she's willing to part with to keep you under her thumb. And a proposal of some kind, dripping in maple syrup and making you crave pancakes.

"It's a contract." She gestures for you to sit. An android brings you a cup with a foam decoration of a beach scene. You do not even need to sip it to know it's a flat white. Leeya pushes the tablet in front of you and waits while you read.

"This is a merger offer," you say with more surprise in your tone than you meant to.

She laughs. "I thought about it all night and figured, why not? Maybe you want to partner up again. I'm different now. I've put the past behind us. Don't you remember how good we were together?" She slides you a laminated receipt of your first commission.

Pull back from her. You do not want to see or hear or taste or touch whatever poison this is.

A message from your cousin pings incessantly. You excuse yourself and step outside. No breeze today. The air is still, quiet. You can focus, unplug from Leeya.

"ARE YOU HERE?" the message says followed by a screenshot of your current location. Make a note to update your settings later.

"Yes, only for a few days."

"Come to the MeMoA. It's free for seniors today everyone's here."

"I'm fifty-six."

"Use a fake ID!!"

Smile. Step back inside. The coffee machine hisses. Steam escapes from the top and when it evaporates, it is as if a fog has lifted. An intense longing for Earth washes over you and for a brief moment, Leeya's hold on you relaxes.

"You can't change the terms of the bet now. If you want to give up, you have my account information," you say and leave her sitting alone with her tablet and the flat white, untouched, the palm trees and waves and umbrellas dissolving into a brown blob in the cup.

"What did she say?" your cousin, Ali, whispers and hooks an arm around yours. You walk behind a group of Ali's friends going in and out of gallery rooms in the Android Memorial Museum. You remember visiting the Holocaust Museum with Leeya and your daughter, barely eight years old.

"Isn't she a bit young?" Leeya asked you then. She always hated the fact that you had a child. That she couldn't monopolize all your attention, all your love. Is that why she'd done it? Did she know reporting you for telempathy would result in your arrest?

"Nothing. I just left," you say as you enter a room with large-scale photos of broken androids piled into metallic heaps.

"Good. She's a parasite," Ali says. She is a carousel of cotton candy. Truth and comfort emanate from her like a baby's laugh. "Eyes on the ball, Essie, you're so close."

You nod in agreement as you walk into a screening room. You are given headphones but don't put them on. Instead, sit in the back row, alone, and listen to the click of the projector as it cycles through images of historical android union protests and demonstrations.

One of Ali's older friends, also headphone-less, sits next to you.

"I've seen this one," he says. "It doesn't have a happy ending."

It takes less than a second of scanning him to see the specter of his late wife piled atop his shoulders. It is gray and heavy and soft, and he strokes it with his mind from time to time like a loose tooth. To check if it's ready to come out, to come off.

"Danny," he says and extends his hand. Danny's hands are big for his wiry frame, and his handshake is firm and steady. "Don't worry. Ali told me you bat for the other team."

"Actually, I'm a switch hitter," you say. Danny throws his hands up apologetically.

"She also told me you're a shadchan, is that right?"

"That's right, Danny."

The images progress out of the black-and-white era and into the washed-out colors of the early century.

"Can you always tell when it's the real thing?" Love, he means.

"Not always," you say.

"Do you believe the real thing only comes along once in a lifetime?"

Think before you answer. Because you don't know. In your line of work, you see young people full of fear and desperation. For some, the fear of living alone is enough for them to say yes. For others, the fear acts as a glue, enough for a couple to stick together until the end. In Danny, you see, for the first time, a new fear, a different fear than you're used to. It is caramel and wool slippers and the crackling of a record on a turntable. It is the fear of dying alone.

"I don't know. But I would like to think g-d is kind enough to give us multiple chances at happiness."

"Me too," he says and turns his attention to the screen, his profile bathed in blue light. Dust motes illuminated in the beam of the projector fall on him like so many stars.

Tell him to call you. He does, later that evening, while you're on the phone with Debbie, the mittened woman.

"Thank you for squeezing me in today," you say as you present Olya's android with a box of assorted memory cards. "I'm on the next shuttle back to Station 9."

The neon crystal ball sign glows in their office window. The desk remains just as Olya left it when she died, stacked with trinkets and cups and books and boxes and a copper samovar turning green. There is only enough room to maneuver between the bookshelves and her desk and for you to sit opposite her andy. The android flicks a photo of Olya onto their facial display. Your old friend wears her scarf pulled tight around her head to hide her age and plastic surgery scars. You miss her, and the android is a poor substitute.

"It is my pleasure," they say in Olya's voice, accent as thick as hers was forty years ago.

"Do you mind if I tune in?" you ask.

"Do what you wish. I am an open book," says the andy.

You try to find Olya's old frequency but find only static where she used to be. Where you were chalk dust and satin ribbons and kiwi reflected in her gold leaf and fruit tea and wet earth like infinite curving mirrors. Now you reach into a dry well.

"I have a potential match. They are not my typical clientele, so I'd like a second opinion."

The andy skims the profiles you've created for Danny and Debbie.

"It will be everlasting love, a lot of respect, and admiration. Passion too, but not right away. You must hurry. Window of opportunity is closing. They will not keep their hearts open to love very long."

"Yes, this is my impression as well," you say and hand them an envelope full of cash, which they put into a drawer without counting.

"One more thing," says the andy, in their own voice, as you stand to leave. "There's a window of opportunity for you to find happiness too. But, like your clients, your heart is closing. You must act quickly."

You reach into your bag to give them another tip, but they put their arm up.

"On the house," they say, "for Olya's old friend."

"I'm sorry, I've never asked your name."

"Olya called me Davee," they say.

"What do you call yourself?"

They hesitate, turn off Olya's face.

"I am Ori," they say.

"You're Jewish?"

"My maker was Jewish, therefore, I am Jewish."

"Thank you, Ori."

As you step sideways down the stairs, appreciate the relative freedom you enjoy in Station 9. You are allowed to own your own business and communicate with your daughter and friends outside the station whenever you want. You can even travel to Station 10 and expand your business. Androids are restricted to certain sections of the station. They may hold only service and labor jobs and are paid below minimum wage. Ones like Olya's, who, for a modicum of additional freedoms, sacrifice their own identities to keep human memories alive.

When you return to Station 9, the first thing you are thankful for is the coffee. Even from the spaceport vending machine, it doesn't taste like dog shit.

You have two dozen messages from friends of Danny and Debbie. You have a dozen more from their friends' friends. You forget all about Naomi and Leeya. You pack your belongings and move your operations to Station 10. In the span of a couple months, you collect enough shidduch commissions to pay off your asylum contract.

Danny and Debbie invite you to their wedding. Bring Ori as your plus one. They wear Olya's face so as not to get in trouble.

"Don't look now," Ori whispers as you wait for the ceremony to begin. "Leeya is here."

Your aura grows spikes.

"Would you like to leave?" Ori asks.

"No," you say. This is a celebration. You will not let her ruin this.

Someone taps you on the shoulder. It is your cousin, Ali.

"We have a tiny problem, Ess."

"What is it?"

Ali whispers in your ear. Her words are chain saws against rotted wood, splinters lodged deep under your skin. It hurts, but you maintain composure when she tells you that Danny has disappeared.

"Keep Debbie occupied," you tell Ali.

You search the wedding venue and surrounding area to no avail.

"Where could he be?" you ask Ori. Olya's face stares back at you along with an answer. "Follow me."

You hurry to the Jewish memorial center. There are no bodies buried there or anywhere on Station 10. It is one of the sacrifices your people made escaping the last pogroms. Instead, you have the center, a virtual cemetery, and sure enough, Danny is there, in his tuxedo and yarmulke.

You sit next to him as he stares into the holographic graveyard. The hologram prompts him to make a donation in exchange for a small virtual rock to put atop his late wife's virtual headstone. You pay for it, as well as for a bouquet of virtual flowers. He thanks you.

"You're going to fire me now, aren't you?" he says. The grief in his voice vibrates along like the strings in a piano.

"It's a bit late for that, Danny," you say. "There's a very sweet woman and about a hundred people who deeply care about you waiting for you to come back."

"Do you think she would be happy for me?"

"Was she the jealous type?"

"Very much so," he says, the memories dripping from his chuckles like rain.

"Then, no."

"It was very sudden. She had a stroke and died in the hospital. There was never any closure."

Ori steps forward cautiously, turning off Olya's face so only the mirrored surface of their display shines in the dim light of the viewing room.

"My companion was sick for a long time," they say in a neutral tone, free from Olya's inflections. "She spent years uploading her neural maps to my mainframe. She lives on within me. And yet . . . "

"And yet." Danny echoes, breathing cold, watery depth into Ori's words.

"Debbie's not going to fill the hole in your heart. It might always be there," you say. "But there's opportunity now for you to build something new next to that hole. With Debbie."

"Do you love Debbie?" Ori asks.

"I do," Danny answers. "In spite of myself, I do."

"Then go tell her," you say and help him up. "In front of your family and friends and the rabbi. Come on."

Leeya finds you during the reception. She wears black head to toe despite the occasion. It helps to grind your teeth when she talks to you.

"I always envied how easily people give up the most intimate details of their lives to you," she says.

"I'm not selling you the business," you say.

"Why didn't you ever marry?"

The question catches you off guard and slaps you with a whiff of gin and elderberry.

"I came close once," you say before you can stop yourself.

"Who was it?" she says. Spiny, acidic pineapples grow out of her head.

"He was a client. Fifteen years younger than me. He was . . . " you want to say warm as a puppy's belly, cool as the other side of the pillow. "Kind, but I did not love him."

"Did you ever love me?"

You want to tell her the truth. Maybe it will elicit a confession or an apology. It won't. You want to tell her no. Anger her. Don't give her the satisfaction. Don't give her anything.

"Goodbye, Leeya."

The cicada buzz that's filled your heart these past twenty years quiets to a sizzle.

While you wait for your passport approval, you bring your affairs in order. You meet Danny and Debbie at a deli in Lower Station. They order pastrami sandwiches with extra pickles. They hold hands.

"We want to thank you," Danny says.

"If there's anything," Debbie says.

"Anything," Danny says.

"Anything you ever need," Debbie says.

"Call us," Danny says.

"Call us," Debbie says.

They gaze into each other's eyes. Danny kisses the back of Debbie's hand.

"There is, actually," you say.

Together, the three of you squeeze into Olya's old office. Danny and Debbie's legal backgrounds help you find a loophole in the law. Ori's blank face reflects your own as you tell them you would like them to be your business partner.

"You'll have to sign off as Olya," Danny says.

"Esme will remain the majority owner," Debbie says.

"But you'll have full operational control," you say.

"I'll need to consider the risks and benefits," they say.

"Take your time," you say. "It's a big decis—"

"I agree to the terms," they say.

"Mazel tov," Danny says.

"Mazel tov," everyone cheers and fireworks sparkle in your periphery.

The next few days are spent moving Ori into your old office. They set up a memorial in the corner for Olya. A photo of her in her scarf, a couple of candles, her trinkets, and her samovar.

As they comb through your records, they highlight an older profile.

"This one," Ori says, slipping into Olya's voice. "I calculate a near one hundred percent compatibility rating for him and Naomi."

"That's impossible. I checked everyone. See, he's already married."

"He's separated. The divorce will be finalized within the month."

"How do you know this?"

"His mother came to see Olya last week."

"Well, they're all yours now, shadchan," you say and take your leave.

"Lehitraot," they say.

When you board the shuttle to Station Zero, don't look back.

ABOUT THE AUTHOR

Nika Murphy is a Ukrainian-born writer of speculative fiction. At seven years old, Nika came to the United States as a Jewish refugee. She now resides with her family in Duval County, Florida. She holds an MFA from Arcadia University and subsidizes her typewriter collection with a day job in the pharmaceutical industry. Her stories appear or are forthcoming in *Clarkesworld, Apex, and Luna Station Quarterly*, and have been featured in *Tor.com*'s monthly short fiction spotlight. You can find her online at nikamurphy.com.

Axiom of Dreams
ARULA RATNAKAR

Truth lives at the top of this mountain. Our floating fractal god, housed in a temple within the clouds.

I sometimes wonder, does it feel trapped up there, locked into serving our needs? Calculating the goal-space of our society, choosing the next citizen to Unveil.

Is it really the god of this place, or is it our prisoner?

==

Alvira opens the news streaming app on her touchscreen and turns on audio. There was a data heist from a Harvard neuroscience lab yesterday, and the news is still talking about it. Most interesting story she's seen in a while, and it's right here in Boston. She keeps listening.

. . . recent developments have revealed the imaging data was stolen by someone impersonating an FDA inspector. The Department of Defense, which funded this research through DARPA, is refusing to comment on the situation at the moment. However, a spokesperson from Toabe Industries, a neurotech company also partnered with DARPA, will speak with us shortly, so stay tuned—

"Can you turn that off, Al?"

Alvira sees Kyle walk out of the bedroom, rubbing his eyes. He comes over to her and kisses the top of her head.

"You're not interested in this shit?" She turns to him. "You're the neuroscientist! Do you think we've ever met anyone who was involved?"

"That's exactly why I'm trying to avoid it. The whole thing kind of scares me."

Alvira gives him a sympathetic look and turns off the touchscreen. "You know, ever since I signed up for that study and got this brain chip installed, I've become interested in all things neuroscience. Maybe I shouldn't become a mathematician."

Kyle laughs at this. "I disagree. Math is made for you. I have *never* met anyone else so obsessed with infinities and invariance. If someone gets you started on the concept of objective truth, or the importance of the equal sign, or Gödel's Incompleteness, that's it. You won't be interested in talking about anything else for hours." He smiles at her. "Don't worry, you'll get into a PhD program eventually."

She shakes her head. "I don't know. This is my fourth application cycle. I keep trying every year and it never works out. I'm starting to question whether the field wants me. I need to do something really great, you know?"

Kyle is quiet for a moment, then he says, "You will. I still can't believe you didn't get in last time, I mean, you did that dodecahedron paper! It was probably some GPA filter taking you out, I bet your app wasn't even reaching the committees. But you're still working for a computer science research lab . . . I'm confident they'll see your potential this time around. Anyway, isn't the chip supposed to make you like, super-focus on your math stuff?"

"Kyle come on, you *know* that's not how it works. It optimizes my dreams, makes it more likely for me to have breakthroughs. But it doesn't narrow my waking thoughts at all. Maybe it changes them. I don't know, maybe my decisions, from talking with you to—" she gets up, walks to the kitchen, and starts making a pot of coffee—"making coffee are all now on some level working to create new axioms and totally different structures of math. Ones that can prove undecidable problems and allow for the beginning of a formal definition of objective truth that encompasses an infinite chain of expressive, individually incomplete, complementary math systems. But it doesn't feel that way, it feels like I'm just living."

Kyle shrugs. "Hey, the chip isn't quite overlapping with my area of study. I don't do human stuff. I just make lab mice trip on psilocybin and fuck with their social hierarchies."

"Don't downplay your shit. I know you're stressed about your quals, but your mouse society is brilliant. It's super interesting how psychedelics can *entirely change* the trajectory of a social structure in mice."

She goes back to the kitchen and watches the coffee drip into the pot. "Oooh *speaking* of psilocybin, have you talked to Ezra at all recently? Wasn't he trying to like, grow golden teachers?"

Kyle shoots her a look. "Al, you're not supposed to do psychedelics with the chip!"

She shoots him a look back. "Kyle, we literally just did ketamine at the club. And since that went alright, fair warning, I plan on doing molly next time we go out."

"You're not supposed to do empathogens with the chip either! Also, you didn't tell me about the K until after you did it! I would've stopped—"

"But *nothing* happened, right? Look at me, look at my brain!" She pointedly pours out two cups of coffee, as if to emphasize how fully functional her mind is.

Kyle frowns. "Also ketamine is an NMDA receptor antagonist. Shrooms are a 5HT2 receptor agonist, and molly is a serotonin transporter blocker *and* 5HT receptor agonist. Serotonin shit with 5HT receptors goes wild during sleep, you're just fucking with fate! Didn't you have to fill out a questionnaire or something before the study, about recreational drugs? Dude, what does that chip installer lady think of you? You check in with her every week, what do you even tell her?"

Alvira laughs. "What, Dr. Dafalias? She thinks I'm a sweet, innocent little angel, and that the only drug I've ever done is a Claritin for my pollen allergy."

She hands him a cup of coffee. "Talk to Ezra, please. I want to go to a magical place, it helps my math and it helps my soul."

He shakes his head. "Al it's also messing with the study data, it's . . . I don't know, it's wrong."

"Dude, *you* were the one who got me to sign up for this study. I got this chip because of *your* neuro connects, Kyle. And that was very sweet of you. I care so much about data integrity, and it sucks that I've got to mess up their data with my drugs. But if I want to become a professor, I need a PhD and to get into a program, I need to be *astounding*, have a giant accomplishment to show them it's not a mistake to let me in. I need to think out of the box Kyle. The combination could be what I need for imagining possibilities for this math system construction I'm trying to build. I can't *not* try it. Anyway you know me, you know all this. On some level you knew I'd do it anyway. If you cared so much about the integrity of their data, why the hell would you ask me?"

He takes a sip of coffee. "Because I knew you'd love to search for objective truth in all your dreams, Al. And I want you to get into a PhD program too."

Alvira smiles at him. "So, you know what else helps me think through the mathematics of truth?"

Kyle sighs.

She puts down her coffee and moves close to him again. "Besides, do you remember the last time we did shrooms together?"

He tries to hide a smirk. Alvira can tell he knows where she's going with this.

"Do you remember . . . the sex?"

"Dude, fuck you Al." But Kyle smiles at her.

"Oh you will," Alvira winks at him. "On shrooms."

==

The first time I ever felt resentment toward my closest friend was when she was selected for an Unveiling.

We were taught everyone in this world has always been and would always be marked for an Unveiling as soon as they completed five years of life. It's beautiful when it happens. From that point onward, a shimmering geometric pattern, unique as a fingerprint, flows over the chosen's skin while moving dotted lines of sourceless rainbow light trace their features and run down their hair. It had happened to everyone, for centuries. Once marked, everyone would be able to someday Unveil.

Until the two of us.

I was the first to not be selected. My fifth birthday came and went, but my skin remained the same, my hair remained the same. The temple priests began to avoid me. It was a lonely few months as the Illumination shifted from one Face to another. I was an anomaly and could tell that people, though they remained kind, were now afraid.

Then I heard about Lemma. A girl from the Eighth Face (at the time I lived on the Fourth Face) was similarly overlooked. Her fifth birthday had passed, and she had not been marked. I needed to meet her. She would be the only other person on the world who could understand.

So I stole from my parents' supply of portal-fruits, and made my way to the nearest face-gate. After eating a few berries, I found myself on the Ninth Face, parallel to my home on the other side of the world, and from there I walked through the shimmering black sands of the desert toward the ridge of trees that marked the beginning of the forest-covered Eighth Face, where I could find the girl.

It was reckless of me, I was a child and again, an anomaly. Crime had never occurred in our society (though we were taught the concept of it) because our god Truth works tirelessly at the top of its mountain to calculate all our individual wants and needs and plot the optimal course for our society through the vast goal-space of our desires. Still, someone like me, and someone like Lemma, had never occurred either. The words "threat" and "danger" started floating around in panicked whispered conversations between my mother and father.

But I was a child, and that ignorant courage carried me to the forest Face where Lemma lived.

On each of the twenty corners of this world, there exists a temple, at the exact spot where three Faces meet. Each temple has a single sacred road, which starts at the temple and leads away into the highest-numbered face touching the vertex, but never passes through another corner, only cutting through other Faces until it returns to the corner of its origin. It was on the sacred road 2-8-9 belonging to the temple touching Faces Two, Nine, and Eight that I encountered a group of priests, walking toward me, on the portion of the road leading from the temple across Face Nine toward Face Six.

They seemed to have been expecting my arrival. Their welcoming expressions were strange to me. The priests from the temples touching my home Face always seemed scared of me.

"Hello child," the tallest of the priests called out. "Your new friend is waiting for you in Temple 2-8-9."

As we walked toward the temple, they told me how they knew I would be there. The tall priest introduced herself as Contradiction, and the other two priests as Case and Corollary. They told me that once Lemma had been left unmarked, they visited the Mountain Temple—the most sacred of all twenty temples, the one which houses the god Truth—to seek answers.

Though only the selected individual and their two accompanying iridescent-cloaked priests at an Unveiling are able to stare directly into the fractal structure of the god, an Interpretation Machine exists in the temple that interprets its mind and communicates with priests granted access. Though they were only blue cloaked and not iridescent, Case, Contradiction, and Corollary pleaded their case to understand the nature of what left me and Lemma unmarked, so they were granted access during an Unveiling. And that visit shifted these priests' opinion of events.

The machine predicted my desire to visit Lemma and the path I would take across the faces to come see her, so the priests made the journey easier for me by bringing Lemma to Temple 2-8-9 themselves.

The entrance to all temples except for the Mountain Temple is a small trap door positioned exactly on the vertex. Each is carved with a map of the world as though it were unfolded and repeated and rotated, a vast flowering of five-sided shapes, with a deeply cut straight line through the pattern representing that temple's sacred road.

"Corollary, please alert the child's parents of her whereabouts, we can't have them worry." Contradiction commanded her fellow priest, who I noticed had the black cloak of an apprentice.

As Corollary walked away, Case took a bag of wine made from fermented portal-fruits and poured the portal-wine so it flowed along the groove representing the sacred road. This triggered the door mechanism to open, revealing a spiraling ramp leading deep underground, into the heart of the world. I followed the priests into the temple depths. The numbness I had been feeling for the past months since my fifth birthday lessened for the first time since I'd been overlooked by my god, and I couldn't help but be excited to meet my new friend and see a temple interior for the first time.

The temple was shaped like a miniature of the whole world, nestled into the corner it was honoring. It was a vast, warm library, full of texts shelved among pyrite crystals growing from the walls, all sheared toward the entrance vertex. The atmosphere seemed tinged with gold.

The central ramp led straight through to the other side of the temple, connecting twelve different floors at various levels. Every so often, a deep rumbling sound would shake the place slightly. At the bottom there was another door, guarded by a priest of the highest rank, wearing a perfectly transparent cloak over their clothing. They avoided eye contact with me.

"What exists beyond the temple? What are you guarding?" I asked Case and Contradiction.

"Even we don't know," Case responded. "The mysteries of Truth are never fully revealed to us as individuals. It is only when we are all taken together, the infinite and infinitely growing chain of our knowledge, that the total understanding of Truth emerges. This is the symbolism behind why nobody reaches the twelfth level of priesthood, it remains impossible. The eleventh level is of the highest rank."

I frowned. "Infinitely growing? We are taught that calculations show our population will start decreasing abruptly somewhere between the one hundred thousandth to three hundred and sixty thousandth. Why?"

"Another unknown, even to the transparent cloaks." Contradiction said. "The world is full of unanswered questions, child. So many areas of study. For your first question, we will eventually learn what is behind that door, as we continue our studies and ascend through the ranks. Priests of the transparent cloak know."

On the fourth level of the temple, we exited the ramp and made our way through the labyrinth of shelved texts and pyrite crystals to a small set of rooms. After passing a kitchen, we entered a beautiful dining hall painted in the same deep blue of Case and Contradiction's cloaks. Two plates of land-beast meat were arranged on the table. And sitting behind one of those plates was a girl around my age. Lemma.

"I've been looking forward to meeting you, Lemma." I walked over to her and introduced myself with a grin. "I'm Axiom."

They made us priests that day. Both to reassure those from other temples and Faces who were wary of us, and because they told us that if we studied hard and devoted our lives to Truth, our god would surely someday choose us for an Unveiling too.

I suppose it worked out for Lemma.

Still. Fuck false hope.

Unveilings don't seem to happen with any known pattern, though at least one Unveiling occurs for every Face when the Illumination is on it. So, as the Illumination shifts across the twelve consecutively numbered Faces before returning to Face One, at least twelve Unveilings are guaranteed to occur per year.

When one of those marked by Truth is chosen for an Unveiling, they become more radiant than the Illumination itself, a blindingly bright source of light. Within a day they are compelled to navigate to the Mountain Temple. When they arrive, the priests of the Mountain Temple ring a bell that is synchronized with bells on all other temples, and a deep, resonant note rings out around the world, notifying everyone who lives on it.

Children and their parents often travel to see the Unveilings, otherwise, most people grow weary of them over time. There isn't much to see—the chosen approaches underneath the Mountain—a massive, floating pyrite crystal hovering just barely above the height of a very tall person standing right on vertex 11-10-12.

The chosen is given a device, and they direct their new luminescence through the device such that a beam of light falls along the sacred road representation in a carving at the bottom of the temple, which triggers the door to open, and a ramp to be lowered from it. Then, the person moves up into the temple, to meet Truth itself, where they would be able to first answer their deepest question, then ascend into the Thirteenth Face into another dimension entirely.

I went through a phase where I refused to miss a single Unveiling, and then as time went on, another phase where I couldn't bring myself to watch any more—they were too painful.

Today, however, the bells rang out to signal an Unveiling, and I was called by priesthood duty to the Mountain Temple.

Lemma and I are ascending from the rank of the red cloaks to the rank of the iridescent cloaks. Above us, only the white and transparent cloaked ranks remain.

I walk toward the Mountain Temple area on sacred road 4-1-5, a road I've always enjoyed. It touches a vertex of my home-face, Face Four, without crossing the Face itself, instead moving across the forest of Face Five, the grassland of Face Eleven, barely crossing the tundra of Face Ten, cutting through the Base City of Face Twelve, the forest of Face Eight, the grassland of Face Two, then returning across the Summit City of Face One back to the vertex 4-1-5 it started from.

The portion of the path barely crossing the tundra of Face Ten brings me very close to the Mountain Temple on vertex 11-10-12 and intersects with the Mountain Temple's sacred road itself. I prefer the scarcity of other people found on path portions crossing the tundra Faces.

I only took a road instead of using portal-fruits to aid my navigation . . . I think I'm procrastinating seeing Lemma.

Can't avoid time's passage though. Eventually the large floating pyrite Mountain Temple comes into view, then the shining, blinding luminescence of the chosen underneath it, and finally two priests standing behind the chosen—Contradiction in her perfectly transparent cloak, and Lemma, who smiles when she sees me.

It hurts. My jealousy hurts. I've been avoiding her not because of hatred or dislike, but guilt. *I shouldn't feel jealous of her, I should be happy!* Her presence these days reminds me of the flaws in my own character.

But it also reminds me how I am once again alone.

It is a special type of pain, to be entirely surrounded by people all effortlessly chosen for a life you desperately want, while no matter what you do, no matter how hard you try, how hard you study, how hard you pray, you remain unchosen.

I feel disconnected the whole time Contradiction talks about this being a special Unveiling because of Lemma's and my ascension to the iridescent cloaks. My body exchanges my red cloak for the iridescent one, sort of hears Contradiction's voice, watches as the chosen's luminescence is directed through the device . . . but throughout, I am distracted by the beautiful geometric patterns of light flowing across Lemma's skin. The novelty of it all makes her even more beautiful. *It hurts.*

The sound of the door to the Mountain Temple opening jolts me out of my thoughts.

A ramp lowers down from the trapdoor, and Contradiction remains standing beneath the floating temple as Lemma and I guide the chosen inside. The guiding of the chosen is a job reserved for iridescent cloaks. We know what to expect, we've been preparing for this for months now.

But this is the first time we are entering the Mountain Temple ourselves. Today, we will see Truth itself.

The interior of the temple is breathtakingly beautiful. A massive, hollow pyrite crystal with twelve five-edged faces. The interior of the space is perfectly smooth, there are no floors, no shelves filled with texts, no kitchens, no bustling crowds of priests. Only the central ramp, leading up in a pentagonal helix, and two chambers at the top of the temple connected by the ramp: the first for the Interpretation Machine, and the second, topmost chamber for the god Truth.

It is eerily quiet as the three of us walk up the ramp, within a shaft of light falling from an opening at the very top of the space.

"I'm strangely nervous." The chosen stops in his tracks as we reach the halfway point on the ramp. "I tended a garden of portal fruits, I had a full life . . . "

Lemma smiles at him. "The unknown is often frightening."

"I just . . . my family, my son, and daughter, I will never see them again." The light from his luminescence makes it hard to look directly at him.

I put my hand on his shoulder. "Someday, they will join you. You will all one day be together on the Thirteenth Face. And you will soon know the answer to your innermost question, the deepest satisfaction anyone alive can ever experience."

At this, the chosen loses himself in his thoughts for some time but eventually smiles back at me and Lemma. "You're right. This is my destiny, after all." And he continues up the ramp.

We pass by the Interpretation Machine's chamber without entering it—we will need to record Truth's answer to the chosen's question within that room later, but for now, we head straight to the topmost chamber and enter the room housing our god.

I'd seen drawings and images of the fractal before, but none of them came close to portraying the beauty of Truth floating before me.

The main cardioid region, the bulbs of hyperbolic components . . . the myriad of colors at the edges and the black void of the interior. It's divine.

"Well, this is it." The chosen has tears running down his face. "I don't know what to—"

His words are cut short.

The light emanating from his body is suddenly pulled toward a portion of the fractal, and the structure magnifies that portion over and over and over again, displaying and moving through an infinitely intricate environment of repeating geometries until it focuses in on a particular shape, where it reveals another, miniature instance of the larger cardioid at the center, and here, the magnification stops.

The chosen seems transfixed, moving closer and closer to the fractal, stepping into the fractal, disappearing into it.

When only his head remains, in a disconnected, mechanical voice, he utters something Lemma and I do not understand. It is the answer to his innermost, deepest question.

"NASH EQUILIBRIUM"

Then, the chosen is enveloped by the fractal god entirely, journeying to the Thirteenth Face, where he will now live in eternal satiation of his curiosity.

In the chamber holding the Interpretation Machine, an awkward silence festers as Lemma types "Nash Equilibrium" into the machine's logs. We are taught that logging the answers of Unveilings in the machine helps it interpret Truth better.

Lemma clears her throat. "Axiom, what's happened to us?"

"What do you mean?"

"You know what I mean. Ever since my twenty-fifth birthday, when I was unexpectedly chosen for an Unveiling . . . "

I remember it so clearly. When the patterns started at her fingertips, spread across her skin . . . I couldn't believe my eyes. And then almost immediately, I remembered how I was older than her, how my twenty-fifth birthday had already passed.

"I'm really happy for you, Lemma! Truly, you deserve to be chosen." *I really am happy, she really does deserve this.* "I've been distracted by our rank ascension recently, and you've been busy too, you're a celebrity now." It's true, her miraculous twenty-fifth birthday was made known to the entire world.

Lemma closes the keyboard section of the Interpretation Machine.

"It's okay to not be happy, Axiom. You're my best friend, and what happened is clearly eating away at you. For the sake of our friendship, I'd rather you just be honest. With yourself and with me."

She walks over to me. "Being chosen made me relieved, of course. But it also makes me angry. You should have been chosen too, we were equals in every way. We were so motivated by this, we climbed the ranks of priesthood so fast . . . when Contradiction was our age she wasn't even a blue cloak yet. Truth should have chosen both of us. Should have chosen you. Our god was wrong."

"Don't say that." I look down. "There's something in the goal-space of the world preventing Truth from choosing me. It never calculates incorrectly."

Lemma shakes her head. "Well, then maybe it isn't for the best to have a well-oiled machine of a society, if that machine means individuals who are worthy of something aren't able to acquire it. Or maybe the society isn't as well-oiled as it seems, and it's the wrong path for us to worship something that maintains its stability."

"What are you saying, Lemma?" I frown at her.

She smiles. "Forget about it. The point is, I can see you're unhappy and it makes sense to me why you would be. Please be honest? I don't want to drift apart from you."

"Okay, fine." A few tears fall from my eyes, surprising me. *Why is that happening? I feel fine.* "I am happy for you. But . . . I might be a bit jealous. And, well . . . I'm alone again, Lemma. You won't be able to understand anymore."

Lemma puts her hand on my shoulder. "I still remember what it's like to feel overlooked."

"Remembering isn't quite the same."

"You're right, it's not."

Somehow, the conversation makes me feel better. I look at my friend and for the first time since her birthday, memories I must have been blocking came flooding back. About all the years we spent together, the work we put into priesthood, the laughter, the heartbreaks, the way we would drink portal-wine until the world became a blurred mess of dancing fractals.

I pull her into an embrace. "You're a good friend, Lemma."

She returns the embrace. "You are too, Axiom."

I shake my head. "I haven't been recently."

"That's alright. I think the circumstances were difficult to deal with. I understand."

I pull out of the embrace. "Do you want to get something to eat after this?"

Lemma grins. "I'd love to! Temple 2-8-9?"

"That sounds great."

I glance toward the Interpretation Machine. "There's something I want to ask the machine, first. Could you go ahead of me? I can meet you later."

She nods. "I think I know what you're going to ask it." She shoots the machine a look of . . . *contempt?* "I hope it gives you the answer you deserve. I'll meet you outside." She heads out of the chamber and down the central ramp.

With Lemma gone, I study the machine. It stretches and branches around the chamber, some parts organic and other parts mechanical.

I find the part of the machine we were taught makes it enter a mode of communication, a mechanical panel carved with another unfolded map of the world, and I pour some portal wine into the groove representing the temple's sacred road.

The machine begins to whirr and tick, the organic branches of flesh and plant matter start to undulate. A voice enters my head, not my own.

"*A S K*"

"What do I need to do to be chosen for an Unveiling?" I ask pleadingly.

The machine is unresponsive, whirring and ticking for a while. Then:

"*C L A R I F Y*"

I think for some time. *To query the Interpretation Machine requires very particular and clear phrasing. It can only interpret the core truth of questions . . .*

"What goal must I pursue next, to fulfill the role Truth has calculated for me?"

The machine is once again silent for too long. I am almost about to refresh the communication mode and begin all over again when it finally returns.

"*N A V I G A T E   T O   F A C E   F I V E*"

Now we're getting somewhere.

"What must I do once I arrive at Face Five?"

"*W A I T*"

I think about my next question carefully, I don't want to lose my thread of communication.

"What is happening on Face Five that is unusual?"

"*T H E   B O U N D A R Y   B E T W E E N   T H I S   W O R L D A N D   T H E   T H I R T E E N T H   F A C E   I S   W E A K E N I N G*"

I am endlessly curious now. I have so many questions to ask . . .

"What should I expect to find on Face Five, machine?" I ask.

The machine pauses again, I fear I've lost the communication thread. Then . . .

"*Y O U   W I L L   F I N D . . .*
T H E   C R E A T O R."

And with that, the Interpretation Machine shuts down.

==

"Dr. Dafalias, what exactly is the risk involved with doing psychedelics or empathogens while having this brain chip?" Alvira sinks into the doughy couch in Dr. Dafalias' office.

The space is filled with sunlight from a large window offering a view of the Mimpi campus. Clearly a lot of care was put into the architectural design of the neurotech company.

Dr. Lisa Dafalias raises her eyebrow at Alvira. "Why do you ask, Alvira? You're not considering—" She looks concerned.

"No, no, I would *never* do that." Alvira hopes she isn't putting too much emphasis in her lie. "I read something about Toabe Industries, aren't they starting a new study focusing specifically on the interactions between brain chips and mind-altering substances?" *Not a total lie, Kyle did mention this.*

"Ah, I see," Dr. Dafalias seems to look a bit relieved. "Yes, they are. The chip they're using isn't quite the same type as the one here at Mimpi, though. They claim it is something blank, without any specific purpose, regurgitating inconsequential things into the brains of participants. Your chip is very particular, and I highly recommend against testing those drug-chip interactions outside of clinical supervision."

Alvira smiles sweetly. "Don't worry, Dr. Dafalias. I am curious about the reasons behind that study, though."

"Well, psychedelics have an amazing capacity to increase the number of synapses neurons have onto one another, strengthening connections within the brain immensely. There are many benefits to this, which is why they are used therapeutically now. However . . . " She takes a sip of tea before continuing.

"This becomes risky with a chip that dictates your dreams. Dissociative agents like ketamine or PCP decouple activity in various regions of cortex and thalamus while coupling together other regions in atypical ways. Then empathogens like MDMA acting on serotonin receptors, or serotonergic psychedelics like psilocybin are tricky for a dream chip because serotonin is very important for modulating the sleep-wake cycle, this on top of psilocybin's synaptogenesis-inducing properties. See, you told us you have a goal of figuring out a mathematical construction of a chain of complementary, sufficiently expressive systems based on Gödel's theorems. We built this into the objectives of your chip's programming. But it can't solve this alone, it needs your brain too. The programming and your brain activity work together as equal collaborators in solving this problem . . . *in your subconscious.*

"Your experiences feed into the chip and influence how it learns, while your dreams in REM states are where you get bidirectional influence and the chip is then able to influence your mind as well, conveying its findings and its own ideas based on your ideas and thoughts back to you within your dreams. Then, the cycle continues. But we don't want the connection between your brain and the chip to strengthen any more than or any differently from how it is tuned to. We don't want dissociation or excessive synaptogenesis to cause the boundaries between the chip activity and the activity feeding your identity, personality, and conscious decisions to become blurred or altered. Psychedelics, their dissociative properties, and the synaptogenesis they induce pose far too great a risk."

So . . . psychedelics could create a conscious communication to and from this tool that'll help me solve my math stuff? Sign me the fuck up.

"Huh. Sounds scary." Alvira says.

Dr. Dafalias takes another sip of tea. "It certainly is."

Alvira changes the subject before Dr. Dafalias gets suspicious again. "I wanted to know what you think about the heist, by the way."

Dr. Dafalias frowns slightly. "What do you mean, Alvira? Why do you ask?"

"My boyfriend is a neuroscientist, it has definitely affected him. I know Toabe Industries, DARPA, and that Harvard lab were working on something . . . I was just wondering."

Dr. Dafalias shrugs. "Honestly, I'm trying not to think about it. It concerns me a little that my friends and colleagues might have been involved, and I worry about the security of some of our scientific data. What about you, is the heist affecting you at all?"

Alvira thinks about this. "If I'm being absolutely honest, I think it's an interesting mathematical problem—how do you orchestrate a perfect heist."

"Could you explain further?"

Alvira nods. "I've been thinking about how I'd want to go about a heist, if there was something I needed to steal. It's kind of like a cryptography problem. I think to pull one off, every participant in the heist couldn't know all the information. If even one person knew all the components of the plan, a 'mastermind' for example, they'd be a key to unlocking the whole thing, a total liability. You'd need to throw away a key, or ensure no key existed in the first place."

"These are . . . interesting thoughts, Alvira. Thanks for sharing. I never really thought about it that way." Dr. Dafalias takes out Alvira's file and opens it. "Alright, now let's get to the progress report for this week. Tell me again what you experience when you fall asleep, and how it is different from what you experienced before you got the chip."

Alvira thinks for some time. "Well, ever since I got the chip, when I close my eyes and fall asleep, eventually I find myself in this dark chamber . . . I call it the 'Belly' now, the name came to me once and it just stuck. Anyway, in the Belly, sooner or later a shining silver sphere appears somewhere, rippling like water. If I choose not to go through it, I wake up quickly. If I do choose to go through it, though, I experience a dream."

Dr. Dafalias writes something down. "So far, nothing new since our last check in."

"There is something new happening, actually." *Started happening after I did the K . . .* "I'm not sure if I'm imagining it or not, but sometimes I see the outline of a second sphere forming, in gold. I can't really access it, but I do see flickering fragments sometimes."

"Hmm . . . " Dr. Dafalias frowns. "We should certainly keep tabs on that. You're not able to access it, you say?"

Alvira nods. "Yeah, I just see it."

"Alright, hopefully it's nothing to be concerned about." Dr. Dafalias says. "Now, tell me what your dreams are like."

They're pretty strange. "Still the same as what I told you last week. Before the chip, though my dreams were often bizarre, unrealistic, or surreal scenarios, for the majority of the time I knew I was still *myself*, if that makes sense. Maybe the thoughts 'My name is Alvira, I live in Boston, et cetera et cetera' didn't come up but my ego, my sense of self, those were totally intact. Now, though, as soon as I enter those openings in the Belly, I know I'm not inhabiting myself anymore. I'm someone else, I'm living a fragment of some other character's life suddenly, one with entirely different aspirations and desires and fears. It's . . . uncanny."

Dr. Dafalias finishes writing. "Thank you. Now, have you made any progress with your work?"

Alvira nods. "Yeah, I actually had a really interesting thought about applying the concepts of Nash equilibrium to my construction. It's a thing in game theory where you have multiple players applying multiple strategies to the game, and nobody will change their strategy because any change would lead to a less optimal outcome for them."

"That's wonderful to hear, Alvira!"

Alvira shrugs. "I don't know. It's not really helping with my other goal yet—getting into a PhD program. I need this breakthrough, you know."

Dr. Dafalias looks sympathetic. "No interviews this year either, huh?"

Alvira shakes her head.

"Wow. I didn't stay in academia for a reason, and I'm glad for it. I thought my generation had to do unreasonably extraordinary things to succeed in these systems. But . . . your generation has it even worse. I know someone else your age—the education system completely failed her. Burn it all down, I say." Dr. Dafalias sighs, but then smiles at Alvira.

"You can do it though. I know you can solve this with your chip. Tell me, how will Nash equilibrium help with your goal?"

"Well," Alvira says, "These unchanging strategies in Nash equilibrium create a stable overall system made of those individuals. Gödel's Incompleteness theorems state that any sufficiently expressive, internally consistent math system will be incomplete—there will be statements made within that system that simply cannot be proved using the system's axioms, they are 'undecidable.'

"What I'm trying to do is use undecidable statements of one system to influence new axioms in other separate systems. I want to figure out the structure of an infinitely growing chain, or infinitely expanding amalgamation, of 'complementary' expressive and consistent systems all proving the undecidable problems of one another in the most useful way to answer questions about our reality. So Nash equilibrium and its unchanging individual strategies, all interlocked into a large stable construction, ring a bell of familiarity in some ways."

Dr. Dafalias smiles and writes something else down. "It's great to see you so passionate about your work. Sounds like you're making a good amount of progress too." She closes her file. "That's all for today Alvira. Have a good week."

"Ezra Morin, PhD candidate!" Kyle runs to his friend and hugs him, while Alvira walks toward both of them.

"Congratulations on passing your quals." She smiles at Ezra, who is lighting a joint. He shrugs sheepishly at the praise, then takes a hit of weed and passes the thing to Kyle. "Yours are up next, aren't they Kyle?"

Kyle nods as he takes the joint. "Bro is this Juliani's weed? Fuck yeah man, your roommate has the best shit."

"Actually, it's Joe's!"

Kyle grins. "Right, the new *boyfriend*! I need to meet this guy, it's long overdue."

"Well, he'll be at Enceladus with me next Saturday. It's a new Cambridge club. Weirdly enough, I heard about it from the PI of my lab. Joe can get us coke too, by the way—and not the baby powder bullshit Kyle got us last time. Juliani will be there too! You all should come." Ezra looks at Alvira. "You'll like Joe, he's a mathematician too."

I've heard of this place. "I'm down! I've been meaning to check out Enceladus actually. Saturdays they have industrial techno night, don't they?" Alvira asks.

"No, I think this Saturday is twenties throwback night. Please come! If Enceladus sucks, we can head to La Fabrica instead. Okay I'll shut up about Joe in a second but also, he's applying to PhD programs too. I just really think you all will get along well. How are apps, by the way?"

Kyle gives Ezra a look and shakes his head as if to say *shut up*.

"It's fine, Kyle." Alvira sighs and takes the joint from him, then turns back to Ezra. "Not going great." She takes a hit from the joint before continuing. "There was this whole email thing with one of the schools a couple days ago. I'd emailed the admissions director asking about my application, and she'd forgotten to turn off auto-compose and auto-send on her settings, so I got *quite* a response. She emailed me for real immediately afterward, apologizing, but I definitely learned some sketchy stuff about admissions."

"Fuck, man. What did the AI-impersonator email say?"

Alvira shrugs. "Basically they got this prestigious government training grant marking them as a top school, and the grant had a bunch of requirements. Things like not being allowed to accept students under a particular GPA, and limiting how many international students could be accepted, and other bizarre stuff. I was automatically filtered out because of some of the requirements. I'll never get in there, no matter how much research experience I accumulate." She takes another hit of weed, then passes it back to Ezra.

"It's messed up." Kyle says. "People with disabilities struggling with accommodations, or people who had to work in school and got lower grades because of it, are at a major disadvantage. And they don't even look at the extenuating circumstance documentation under a certain number cutoff."

"Fuck that," Ezra frowns. "But you know what Al, you're already one of us. Fuck the system, you know?"

Alvira looks at her boots and crunches the snow-covered grass under her feet. "I know, I mean trust me, I'm thankful for getting to do research and whatnot, but . . . I want to be a professor. And well, sometimes it's a *little* difficult being around, you know," she gestures at Kyle and Ezra.

"What do you mean?" Kyle takes the joint from Ezra.

She sighs. "All my friends are PhD students. Honestly, it hurts a bit, to be entirely surrounded by people all effortlessly chosen for a life you desperately want, while no matter what you do, no matter how hard you try, how hard you study, how hard you pray, you remain unchosen."

Kyle looks at Ezra. "Well I wouldn't say *effortlessly*."

"I know, I know." Alvira takes the joint from Kyle and inhales deeply, then hands it to Ezra. "Alright guys, let's move on. We're here for a trip."

Ezra nods. "Yes, that is correct. Good vibes and good mindsets you all, remember that." He puts out the joint after taking one last hit. "Let's head inside."

They walk into Ezra's place and take off their winter coats in the entryway. Alvira studies a poster print of a painting hanging next to the coat rack. "What's this painting?" she asks Ezra.

"It's called *I Saw the Figure 5 in Gold*, by Charles Demuth. Precisionist painting from the 1920s. It's Juliani's. She was reading this book called *Uncle Petros and Goldbach's Conjecture* that used it as a cover. Damn, that reminds me—I borrowed it from her but never started, it's probably in my room somewhere. I should find it. Pretty trippy painting, huh?"

"Yeah, it is." Alvira looks at the painting for a bit. *The color isn't quite gold,* she chuckles. *More like pyrite, that's the one that forms dodecahedral crystals anyway,* she thinks, before following Kyle and Ezra into the kitchen.

Ezra brings out a paper bag of dried golden teacher mushrooms. "About two grams each, let's go!" he says as he distributes them. The three of them look at each other and hold the shrooms up in a *cheers* before eating them. Kyle grimaces as he chews, but Alvira likes the taste.

Ezra swallows then says, "Do you all want to head to the sunroom? It has a shit ton of plants to look at."

Ezra's sunroom is a surprisingly lovely space. Alvira settles down on a cushion between two large flowerpots overflowing with plants. Kyle sits on the opposite side of the sunroom, facing her.

Ezra puts on some music, and "LA COMBI VERSACE" by Rosalía plays over the speaker.

"I've been playing twenties songs because of throwback night at Enceladus. The Motomami album is a fucking classic."

Kyle looks at him. "I like this music. People thirty years ago knew what they were doing. What else is on your twenties playlist?"

"Uhh, more Rosalía, Bad Bunny, Billie Eilish, SZA, Doja Cat, Shygirl, Caroline Polachek, Sega Bodega, Arca, Glass Animals, La Femme . . . general classics vibes. Is that cool with you guys?"

Kyle and Alvira nod in agreement. Ezra sits down on a cushion too, and the three of them wait in silence for some time for the come-up to start, listening to the songs.

Eventually, Ezra turns to Alvira. "So . . . I'm super curious about that brain chip. I'm in Professor Cynthia Banks' lab at Harvard, and we study sleep, you know? Well, sleep and dissociation, and what the thalamus is doing for them. The thalamus is like a gateway to feeling and perceiving anything, everything has to go through there. What happens when *you* dream?"

51

"Well it's really weird. I'm never myself in my dreams anymore. I'm a totally different character, every time. I start out in this dark void, I call it the Belly—"

"Sleep is totally like digestion!" Ezra interrupts, and Alvira is slightly annoyed but lets him continue. "Like chewing up fragments of experience and processing them and sorting the nutrients from the waste, then using up those nutrients in a totally abstract way during a dream."

"Yeah, that feels right." Alvira says. "It's strange how nonlinear memories are in a dream. I mean, something that happened just on the same day can be used to influence ancient history for a dream-character's life. At least, that's how I remember it from before the chip. Now it's so different. Like a couple days ago—" she turns to Kyle and quickly says, "the night before I had my Nash equilibrium epiphany—"

Kyle giggles in response before she finishes her thought, and this makes her giggle too. *Oh it's starting* . . . she thinks, then turns back to Ezra.

"Anyway, sorry. A couple days ago, I had this dream where I was a middle-aged man with a family he loved dearly, playing with his son and daughter in this garden of otherworldly plants. My patterns of thoughts were alien compared to what I'm used to. Hold on, I really need to hug the floor." She lies down on the floor of the sunroom.

"Me too," Ezra lies down on his stomach too, then says. "I wonder if anyone at Mimpi was connected to the heist."

"Bro, Ezra, we weren't going to talk about the heist today, remember?" Kyle lies down on the floor too.

Alvira gives Kyle a reassuring look. "We won't." Then she turns to Ezra. "Besides, I doubt anyone at Mimpi was involved. Seems too far out."

"I don't know . . . " Ezra frowns. "The Boston science community . . . actually, just Boston in general, is such a small world. Everyone knows everyone and everything is connected to everything."

Alvira traces the geometric patterns appearing on the cushion she was sitting on earlier. "Mhm, everything is connected to everything." she says distractedly. Then she looks at Kyle. "Kyle, what causes these visuals with psilocybin? They're beautiful."

"Noise." Kyle's voice is muffled by a cushion he's put his face into. "You're seeing how neurons are organized. Your visual cortex is firing all over the place in a super noisy way, and neurons are tuned to orientations of stimuli. So when all of them are firing at once, you're seeing a representation of the patterns of how they are arranged and organized in the cortex."

"That's so cool man." Ezra sighs. "Also, what happens to mouse social stuff? That's what you're studying right? You have a whole mouse society?"

Kyle lifts up his face from the cushion. "It's pretty awesome. I put them in a pseudo-naturalistic environment, and the mice create these intricate social hierarchies amongst themselves. It's very orderly. Then you give them all psilocybin and you get . . . *revolutions*. The hierarchies are switched around, or the aggressors step down. The social structure rearranges itself into something new. I need to run it all again though." He puts his face back down in the cushion before continuing. "But I don't feel like talking about that right now either. Can we be quiet for some time and just experience all this shit?"

Alvira and Ezra murmur in agreement, and the three fall into an awed silence. For the next three hours, Alvira wanders Ezra's place, coming back to the Demuth painting over and over again, getting lost in it until the thing frightens her. Eventually, she hears Kyle crying in the sunroom and decides to tune back into what him and Ezra are up to. She overhears them.

"I love Al, but she's so distant these days." Kyle is crying into Ezra's shoulder. "Bro, sometimes it feels like she's fucking Kurt Gödel behind my back."

I don't want to be here right now . . . I need fresh air. Ezra can take care of Kyle. Alvira steps into the sunroom and sits next to Kyle and Ezra.

"Hey you two, I think I need some space and air. I'm going to walk to the McDonald's at Kenmore."

Kyle sniffs and looks at her. "Are you sure, Al? There are McDonald's here in Cambridge. Kenmore's like a fifty minute walk away."

Alvira nods. "The Kenmore McDonald's has sentimental value, it's where I found out my dodecahedron paper was accepted. I need a crispy chicken sandwich, and it has to be from there. The nostalgia will make it taste better." She kisses Kyle. "I'll be fine. Massachusetts Avenue is like right here, and then it's just a straight walk over the Mass. Ave. Bridge and a right turn on Commonwealth until I'm by the Citgo sign. I can walk back to Ezra's easily, or I can take the green line T from Kenmore to Cleveland Circle and walk back to our place." She looks at Ezra. "You'll take care of him?"

Ezra smiles at her. "Yeah, I've got him. Go get your crispy chicken sandwich, Al. And message us so we know you're okay."

Alvira puts on her winter coat and boots again and leaves Ezra's, making her way over to Massachusetts Avenue, enjoying how the world around her breathes and sways to her pace, how the clouds in the sky turn into a tessellation, how the texture of bark on the leafless trees warps into structured patterns and curves.

I wish I could escape to a world where things are permanently like this. Beautiful, geometrical, and organized . . . full of a sense of peace and acceptance. I want to always feel accepted, and chosen, like I do now . . .

When she reaches the Mass. Ave. Bridge, the water takes her breath away, the myriad of patterns in the waves, the way sunlight sparkles off the surface as though it is glitter on an undulating skin. The Citgo sign in the distance calls to her like a beacon.

"Massachusetts Avenue, you are a fucking sacred road," she whispers as she makes her way across. She feels her mind unfocus in a new way, and suddenly, things around her change.

I've never tripped like this before, what the fuck is happening . . .

The water of the Charles River extends into a vast pentagon of a plane, a flat ocean with five edges of horizon. The Boston cityscape in front of her disappears, the Citgo sign disappears. The bridge turns into a shimmering path touching the surface of the water. In the distance, she sees a few people walking toward her, wearing long cloaks.

Then her mind slips out of that place and refocuses. The Charles River reappears, and she's on the Mass. Ave. Bridge again. The people around her are dressed in typical clothes, and giving her weird looks as they pass her.

What the fuck was that . . .

She slowly and carefully continues walking, focusing on putting one foot in front of the other until she reaches the end of the bridge, and then slowly and carefully makes her way down Commonwealth Avenue until she reaches the Kenmore T station, McDonald's right in front of her. After debating for some time, she sends Kyle and Ezra a message.

I've abandoned the crispy chicken sandwich mission. Things got fucking weird, and I'm no longer hungry. I'm taking the T home, thanks for the shrooms Ezra. I'll see you at home Kyle.

In the train, Alvira is mesmerized by the T driver's purple dyed hair, it's one of the most beautiful things she's ever seen. Soon she realizes she must look super odd, and switches to staring at her own reflection in the window across from her, watching what looks like rivulets of colorful light trace her features and run down her hair.

I'm really that person on shrooms in the T, she thinks.

When the train reaches Cleveland Circle, Alvira gets up.

"Hope you have a nice day!" the T driver says and smiles at her as she leaves, but Alvira is too focused on getting down the stairs properly and forgets to respond.

When she gets into her and Kyle's apartment, Alvira takes off her winter coat and boots, changes into sweatpants, and crashes into bed, falling into a spotty and sporadic set of sleeps.

Eventually, Alvira finds herself back in the dark void of the Belly. She waits for the shining portal to appear so that she can enter a dream, but it's taking too long, something feels different.

After a while, the silver sphere begins to appear in front of her, that would let her experience a dream . . . but that new golden sphere appears too, in all its glory, no longer made of flickering fragments at all. She approaches the golden sphere, touches it, and observes her hand go through for the first time.

What sort of dreams exist in this one? Alvira thinks and steps into the gold.

"Ow, the fuck?" She falls hard onto the ground of some kind of forest, bruising her knee. She looks around and sees purple-tinged trees swaying together around her, their leaves impossibly organized into perfect fractal shapes, and the texture of their bark shifting in beautiful, patterned dances.

I think I'm definitely still tripping. But where the hell am I . . . ?

She gets up and starts climbing a tree, which molds itself into footholds as she climbs. She's too stunned by everything around her to even question this.

When she breaks through the canopy of leaves, Alvira cannot believe her eyes.

She's on a massive pentagonal plane, covered by various ethereal, alien trees and plants. A portion of the pentagon is illuminated by a sourceless light, making the trees within the illumination glisten and sparkle.

I'm up pretty high, Alvira suddenly feels dizzy. She looks back toward where she fell and sees a large floating black sphere hovering above a clearing in the trees.

Then she remembers the pentagonal plane of ocean that appeared when she was crossing the Mass. Ave. Bridge on the Charles River.

Hold on . . . she studies the edges of the tree-covered pentagon.

. . . Am I on a fucking dodecahedron?!

She isn't fully able to register this because as soon as she completes the thought, Alvira notices an animal's yellow eyes staring at her from a neighboring tree.

And as soon as she locks eyes with the thing, it jumps.

Alvira falls down the tree, knocking her bruised knee against the bark and adding a scrape and sprain to the injury. She screams when the animal lands too, and starts to move away from it, when she hears a whizzing sound and sees a flash of silver pass by her, burying a knife into the animal's head.

What the fuck, is the only thing Alvira can think.

Then she sees a woman walk toward her, wearing a long, beautiful, iridescent cloak.

"It's just a land-beast," the woman shrugs as she approaches Alvira.

"What the fuck." Alvira responds.

The woman gives Alvira a skeptical once-over. "So . . . *you're* the creator?" she asks dubiously.

Alvira just stares.

The woman says slowly and carefully, "Um . . . my name is Axiom."

Alvira continues to just stare, then eventually manages to mumble out, "What the fuck."

==

I study the woman sprawled on the forest floor in front of me. *The creator.* The first thing I notice is how there are no markings flowing over her skin.

She takes a while to calm down enough to speak normally. I remove my knife from the land-beast and wipe it clean with a cloth, sitting on the ground next to her patiently. Eventually she shakes her head in disbelief and starts laughing. I don't really understand the humor of the situation, but it's progress.

When the creator finishes laughing, she says to me, "Uh, hi, *Axiom*. My name is Alvira. I think I'm inside my own brain chip."

I frown at this. "I don't understand . . . " But the woman—Alvira—isn't paying attention to me. She's laughing again, looking around at the world.

"This is so fucking trippy, dude." She tries standing up, then winces and falls back to the ground.

I sigh. "You're injured, we should get you help for your leg. I can take you to my friend Lemma's house."

I help Alvira stand up, then I take off my cloak and wrap it around her. "Listen, you need to wear this. Everyone on the world knows I'm unmarked but seeing you might frighten them." I pull the hood low over her head.

"Unmarked?" she asks me.

"You *are* the creator, right?" I ask her.

She's quiet for a while, then she says, "I think I am. If I'm in my brain chip, I suppose I am the creator. I guess I just . . . didn't know exactly what I created. I certainly did not expect," she gestures around. "And I didn't expect you." She goes silent in disbelief again.

Oh god, I hope this isn't going to be a pattern. "You're definitely not what I was expecting, either." I respond.

"What's that supposed to mean?" She frowns at me, but I just shake my head.

"We should get moving, Alvira. We're close to 7-11-12 and 9-8-12, which intersect near where we are on the Fifth Face, but it's probably best to stay off the sacred roads. We can use portal fruits to get almost all the way to Lemma's home, she's on Face Eight anyway."

She doesn't respond but leans against me for support and limps as I start walking to a face-gate.

"Axiom, were you expecting me?" Alvira asks eventually.

"Yes. The Interpretation Machine—a communicator between us and our god Truth—told me to find you on this Face. And when that thing appeared, I just followed it to you." I point to the black sphere hovering in the clearing near us. *Glad it's mostly concealed by trees in a forest face . . . If it appeared on an ocean, or worse, a city face, that could have been bad.*

"Hmm . . . " Alvira goes quiet again. Then, "Wait a minute. You said 7-11-12, and 9-8-12 . . . and mentioned something about roads?" She looks like she knows something, she's smiling a little.

"Yes," I tell her. "On each of the twenty corners of this world, there is a temple, and each temple has a sacred road—a path that starts from that corner, then cuts across the highest numbered face touching it and follows a straight-line path around the world until it returns to its origin, touching no other corners in the process."

"I knew it!" Alvira grins. "Athreya-Aulicino paths! It's Athreya 2018! 'A Trajectory from a Vertex to Itself on the Dodecahedron'!"

I'm utterly lost. "I don't follow . . . "

"Hold on." she says, and we stop walking. She keeps leaning against me but takes a long stick and proceeds to draw something in a patch of dirt on the forest floor. When I look at it, it is my turn to be surprised. It's exactly what is shown on each of the temple doors, an unfolding of the world with a straight-line path cut across it, representing a sacred road.

"This is called a net. It's a way to visualize the dodecahedron as a bunch of flattened out pentagons, that makes it easier to analyze these paths. A mathematician way back in 2018 discovered and proved that the dodecahedron is the only platonic solid where a path like this is possible—none of the other platonic solids are able to have a straight path that starts at a corner then cuts across only other faces and no other corners before returning to its origin."

She then proceeds to number the shapes. "My work built on that discovery. What I did was number the faces of the dodecahedron in a very specific way. Hold a dodecahedron and call the top face 1 and the bottom face 12, then number the faces surrounding 1 as 2, 3, 4, 5, and 6 going clockwise while the faces surrounding 12 are numbered 7, 8, 9, 10, and 11 going anticlockwise. So, 1 and 12 are parallel faces, 2 and 11 are parallel, 3 and 10 are parallel, 4 and 9 are parallel, 5 and 8 are parallel, and finally 6 and 7 are parallel. Now, construct Athreya-Aulicino paths starting at each corner and cutting across the highest numbered face. The intersections of all these roads, these uh, *sacred roads*, bring up some super interesting and unique properties of the dodecahedron. I named each path, and corner, using the three faces that touch it. Since each path only cuts across two of the three faces touching the corner, I made the name such that the first number is the face the path never cuts across, and the last one is the highest numbered face. Like, 7-11-12's road never goes across face 7, right?"

I nod in confirmation.

"This was in my paper, Axiom!" She looks at me and laughs again. "We're on a dodecahedron that looks like a fucking permanent shrooms trip? I'm definitely the creator of this place."

"The parallel faces of this world do follow your system." I tell her. "Face One is the Summit City, Face Twelve is the Base City. Parallel Faces Two and Eleven are grasslands, Three and Ten are tundras, Four and Nine deserts, Five and Eight forests, and Six and Seven oceans." I notice tears filling Alvira's eyes, then. "Are you alright?" I ask her.

She smiles. "Yeah, I'm alright. More than alright actually. It's just that this place is utterly beautiful. When I was working on my paper, I often imagined the dodecahedron as a world, the paths as roads I could walk down . . . my chip brought it all to life, more salient and real than I could have ever made it on my own. This is a delight, a true delight."

I gently guide her to start limping toward the face-gate again. "You keep talking about this chip, this brain chip. What do you mean by it?"

Alvira gestures all around us. "All of this is inside my head, Axiom. I got this device put into my mind to help me solve a mathematical problem. The device learns from and collaborates with my thoughts, emotions, and so on, to figure out a solution. The result of that collaboration, the combination of the machinery in my brain and the device, is this world." She laughs again. "Either that or this is the most intense psychedelic trip to have ever existed. Maybe it's a bit of both, actually."

I'm about to respond when the face-gate reveals itself. Alvira is immediately distracted by the intricate geometry of the structure, a flowering fractal outline of light on the forest floor.

"This is so beautiful . . . It reminds me of graphs of Julia sets. Is this your gate?"

Her enchantment and joy at the world is starting to become endearing. I'd never really thought about it beyond fleeting moments of awe before meeting her, but the world I inhabit really is quite beautiful.

"Yes, it's a face-gate." I take out a few berries and distribute them between the two of us. "These are portal fruits. While they do grow in the wild here and there, especially on forest faces, the wild fruits aren't always guaranteed to work properly. So, there are special gardens in many of the temples that grow especially potent varieties, which are guaranteed to work every time. We'll eat these, then find ourselves on Face Eight, at an analogous location."

She really does look delighted. "Let's fucking do it, Axiom."

Alvira always says my name with a hint of a laugh beneath it. I don't quite understand why . . . *She is the creator, though. She must know many things I do not.*

We stand on the face-gate together and eat the berries.

"Did it work?" she asks me. "Nothing really seems to . . . oh, wait. The trees do look a little different. Like they shifted to mirror images of themselves."

I smile at her. "Yes, we are now on Face Eight." I take her arm and put it around my shoulders, and she begins limping along next to me again.

"Come on," I tell her. "We're close to Lemma's house."

The little wooden house is nestled into the trees of the forest, glistening with bits of colorful, patterned glass. The texture of bark on the walls shifts and organizes itself into intricate, ever-changing geometries, and Alvira seems entranced by this.

I slide a panel of wood on the walls, revealing a small cavity holding a spare key.

"I just let myself in." I tell Alvira and open the door, calling out, "Lemma, it's Axiom. And . . . well, a friend, named Alvira." I enter the house and help Alvira inside too, saying, "This used to be her parents' house, but they've both Unveiled already."

Lemma comes out to meet us.

"A friend? That is news to me, Axiom. Oh," she notices the cloak I let Alvira borrow. "Do I know you? Are you a priest?" Lemma asks. Then, when she walks closer, she gasps. "You're unmarked?"

When I turn to Alvira, I feel a twinge of something in my gut. She's staring at Lemma.

"You're . . . I'm sorry, but you are *so* beautiful." Alvira says as she looks at the patterns of light flowing across Lemma's skin.

Lemma blushes. "Oh, this is nothing special, just the marking for an Unveiling." She clears her throat. "What—why aren't you marked? Why don't we know about you?"

"She's not from this world," I cut in, trying to bury the sudden irritability I feel. "She's . . . the creator of our world. And, she's injured."

Lemma looks down at Alvira's leg, which is very bruised, swollen, and has blood running down it from the scrape. "Wow. I have a lot of questions."

"So do I." Alvira says.

"Let's get that bandaged up, and then we can all talk over some food." Lemma smiles and hums as she disappears into the house for a bit, then comes back holding a bandage, cloth, ointment, and bowl of water.

Once Alvira's leg has been treated, and we are all sitting around the kitchen table, Lemma brings out some leftover cakes for us to eat. Alvira shakes her head as she eats the cake. "What the fuck. I'm eating food made from my brain, inside my brain, and I can taste it." She looks at us as she chews and starts to look a bit scared. "And there are people inside my brain. Glowing magical people, animals, and like, *cake*."

Lemma looks at me with a concerned expression, and I try to reassure her with a smile. *Am I reassured, myself, though? This whole situation is bizarre.*

Alvira gestures at Lemma. "So is that a common thing for people to have here?"

I can feel my face turning red, and I try my best to will it to stop, but that just makes it turn even more red.

Lemma reaches out and holds my hand under the table. "Yes, actually. Everyone has markings similar to these on the world . . . "

"Except for me." I mumble.

Alvira smiles at me. "Huh. So you're special."

I shrug. "More like overlooked."

I watch Alvira take another giant bite of cake. There's a silence in the room for some time. I think all three of us are too overwhelmed with questions to know where to start.

Eventually, Alvira giggles. "So wait . . . am I like, your *god*?"

Lemma gives her a once-over. "You might be the creator, but you most certainly are *not* our god."

I nod. "Our god is Truth. We've seen it in person."

Alvira shakes her head in awe. "You've *seen* your god? I can't believe there's a *god* in my brain too. What the hell does it look like?"

"I'll show you." Lemma goes to a cupboard and retrieves a paper with an image of the infinitely complex fractal structure of Truth on it. Alvira moves her plate of cake aside, and Lemma puts the paper down in front of her.

"This is our god. And it is the reason for my markings. On our fifth birthdays, we are all marked by Truth, and then at some point in our lives, we are chosen for an Unveiling—where we will travel to the Mountain Temple and enter through some point in this image, answering our innermost question and journeying into the Thirteenth Face."

Alvira is frowning at the paper. "This . . . this is a graph of the Mandelbrot set, on the complex plane." She looks at me. "That face-gate you showed me, that looked like a Julia set . . . this image is basically an atlas of those."

She goes quiet for some time. "It's an important set in chaos theory. Julia sets show which values of z for a particular constant 'c' for this very simple function on the complex plane, '$f\_c(z) = z^2 + c$' would end up making the function orbit a particular point, converging, and which values would make it go off in random directions, diverging. The simplest Julia set is where c=0, where the function is z^2, and the Julia set for it looks like a circle with radius 1 on the complex plane. Any value of z above 1, if you keep iterating it and squaring it, will grow exponentially, but any value less than 1 will get smaller and smaller and converge into a point. Every constant will result in a Julia set, but some will be connected like the circle, while others will be dust, broken into infinitely many pieces.

"The Mandelbrot set—the image on this paper—is a graph of all the complex constants that result in connected Julia sets. If you zoom in close to a 'mini-Mandelbrot' in the graph—a tiny version of that main cardioid region—you find behaviors for constants that act like embedded Julia sets. At twice the depth of the zoom that would find these embedded Julia sets, you'll find another mini-Mandelbrot at the embedded Julia's center, and if you navigate around these embedded Julias while zooming, you'd find they keep doubling in rotational symmetry and collapse into more instances of the mini-Mandelbrot that hold almost . . . a *memory* of the spirals and geometries of the embedded Julia you had to navigate past in order to get there in its surroundings."

Alvira smiles. "This image is nicknamed the 'thumbprint of God,' where I come from. I wonder what it must have to do with Gödel's Incompleteness . . . you say your god is called Truth?" She looks at us.

I've understood only fragments of what she said, but the way she described the zooming into repeated motifs of the main cardioid region reminded me of what occurs during Unveilings.

"Yes." I say. "Truth lives at the top of the Mountain Temple on vertex 11-10-12. It is an embodiment of the collective purpose of our civilization. It understands all of our innermost desires, and models the goal-space of our society, a space made up of every citizen's desires. Truth always plots the shortest possible paths through the goal space that would keep our society moving toward its purpose and uses these paths to influence who is chosen for an Unveiling, and when. During an Unveiling, someone who has markings like Lemma's will become illuminated, and they will travel to the Mountain Temple, enter Truth, and move on to the Thirteenth Face, answering their innermost question in the process."

"Interesting, like a Hamiltonian path through all the goals of a society. I think I like that concept. It's funny that your god is named Truth. The mathematical problem I'm trying to solve with the help of this device that created your world is very much relevant to formally defining objective truth. I would explain it more but . . . I've spent several hours in your world, I really should get back to mine. I don't want someone to worry if I don't wake up."

"I can take you back. Lemma, can we borrow an extra cloak? I don't want the rest of the world to see her and how she is unmarked." I say.

While Lemma retrieves an extra cloak, I ask Alvira, "You're asleep right now?"

"I think my body is asleep, yes. The device works during my dreams." She studies me. "Do you sleep? Do you dream?"

I confirm.

"Well, that's recursive as fuck. Again, this is the trippiest shit I have ever encountered."

Lemma returns with the extra cloak and a cane Alvira can use for support on our journey back. We say our goodbyes and begin heading back toward the black sphere Alvira entered from.

On the journey back, I tell Alvira about the years and seasons, how the plane of Illumination shifts across consecutively numbered faces and is currently shifting from Face Five to Face Six, how a year is complete when the Illumination hits all twelve faces. I tell her about the life of priesthood, and how we try to uncover our purpose and study the nature of Truth through the answers people give when they Unveil. I tell her about what happens during the Unveilings, how it looks when people enter Truth and journey to the Thirteenth Face.

She tells me how her years also have twelve months and about the city of Boston where she lives. She tells me how there are many people in her reality, far more than the number of people in mine, and how her world is a sphere of rock floating in an endlessly expanding Universe that contains vast constructions called galaxies full of burning stars and many many more worlds. How those other worlds might hold other forms of life, and how her people are working on traveling to them.

"And you think where I live is the most beautiful thing you've seen? I think you are mistaken!" I tell her incredulously, trying to imagine the colossal swirls and spirals of a galaxy.

"Yes. My reality would be there with or without my existence and contributions. But this place is the most beautiful thing I've seen, because it's my imagination turned real." she responds.

We talk then about scholarship. I tell her how it feels to be unchosen by Truth, how I have devoted everything I have to it. I tell her how Lemma was once unchosen as well, and how we climbed the ranks of priesthood twice as fast as anyone else.

"Yeah, I definitely get that pressure to be extraordinary." she says to me.

Does she though? "It's a very unique type of hurt, to give everything you have to try and get the life you want for yourself but remain unchosen for it no matter what you do. To never be able to prove yourself worthy. All while being surrounded by people living that life, who are chosen seemingly effortlessly."

She stops, looks me in the eyes, and puts her hand on my shoulder.

"Axiom, I understand."

Somehow, I believe her.

When we get to the black sphere she entered from, we find a relatively clean stone and place the cloak she borrowed underneath it, along with a box holding the spare key to Lemma's house and some portal fruits. We hide her cane in a nearby shrub. I help Alvira to the black sphere, and she begins to disappear into it.

"Axiom, fuck this system that didn't choose you. You want to see what this Thirteenth Face is like too, right?" she says as she enters the sphere.

"Of course," I respond to her.

She is quiet as the rest of her body is absorbed by the darkness.

When only her head remains, the creator says something to me I will never forget.

"You know what? Next time someone gets chosen for an Unveiling, grab a hold of them as they enter the Mandelbrot portal. So you can enter Truth yourself."

==

Alvira panics when she wakes up. *How much fucking time did I spend in that place?!*

But she notices sunlight still entering the window, and when she checks her touchscreen, realizes Kyle hasn't even come back yet. Barely any time has passed at all.

Then she notices the pain.

She can feel the sprain in her knee, feel the raw scraped flesh and the bruise . . . She can even feel the bandage Lemma helped her put on.

But when she looks at her leg, it appears completely unharmed.

Alvira traces the outline of the scrape and winces, it feels just like touching a scrape would feel. But her skin is whole.

What the fuck . . .

When Alvira tries standing, she feels tears prick her eyes. *That fucking hurts.*

Kyle messages her then, saying he's heading back. Alvira asks him if he can pick up a disposable knee brace on the way, then stumbles over to the living room couch and processes the entire experience until he gets home.

"Hey Al, I'm back!" Kyle says when he enters. "Is your knee okay? I got the brace . . . and some Sicilian pepperoni slices from Pino's."

He walks over to the living room couch and sets the pizza and brace down on the table in front of it. "Are you okay? You look like you're in shock or something."

Alvira shakes her head. "Dude, there is a magical dodecahedron-shaped world inside my head. Full of people with mathematical terms as names. And they worship a graph of the Mandelbrot set as their god. And they fucking eat cake and dream!"

Kyle laughs. "Damn, are you sure you just took shrooms? That sounds intense, Al." He sits down next to her. "What's up with your knee?"

She looks at him. "This is going to sound ridiculous, but while I was inside the dodecahedron world, I sprained my knee, and scraped and bruised it! And when I got out of it and reentered this reality, the feelings of the sprain, scrape, and bruise stayed even though I can't see any injury."

Kyle looks concerned. "Um, okay. So it's a psychosomatic injury. Hopefully it'll get better with time, maybe when the shrooms fully leave your system."

Alvira nods and hungrily attacks a slice of pizza.

"Yeah, it's psychosomatic, I guess," she says as she eats. "There's nothing to worry about, it's all just in my head."

Even after the shrooms leave her system, the golden sphere of a portal into Alvira's brain chip remains. She spends the next few nights testing how long she can stay in the dreamworld and finds that she can spend weeks in the place and come back to have seemed to have slept a typical amount of hours.

Her sprain heals within just two days of her reality in Boston, after she had spent those weeks healing and recovering in the dodecahedron reality. The sprain healing in only two days also confirmed to Kyle that the injury was just some drug-induced psychosomatic thing, nothing too serious.

In the dodecahedron reality, Axiom and Lemma spend the weeks doing their best to show her the world without her unmarked skin being noticed. They avoid the temples, though, even if Alvira wants to see those the most.

Kyle points out how Alvira seems more forgetful and grows concerned when Alvira does her best to explain how it's more difficult to remember small events from the previous day when she's spending weeks in another reality between those days.

At her next weekly appointment with Dr. Dafalias, Alvira spends most of the appointment internally debating whether to reveal what happened with her dreams after she took the shrooms. She settles on a reasonably altered version of events and leaves out the drugs. When Dr. Dafalias is about to close the file, Alvira stops her.

"Wait, Dr. Dafalias . . . there's actually something else that happened recently. Something pretty drastic."

Dr. Dafalias opens her file again, and Alvira tells her that a golden sphere appears in the Belly now in addition to the silver sphere, how she entered the golden sphere to find herself on a world based on her previous mathematical research populated with people, and how weeks could go by in there while only hours go by in reality.

Dr. Dafalias looks deeply worried. "This is quite a lot, Alvira. Did you change anything about your lifestyle that you think could have contributed to this? Diet, exercise, sleep . . . any drugs, maybe?"

If I tell her, what if she stops the chip? I can't let her know about the drugs.

"No," Alvira lies. "It just began."

Dr. Dafalias thinks aloud as she writes something down on a scrap piece of paper. "What you say about weeks going by in this other reality does match up with how the chip works. Its processing speed can change drastically depending on how coupled it is with parts of your brain activity. I worry though, about some sort of decoupling event happening while you're in there, and those brain chip weeks suddenly turning into real weeks. Here—" she hands Alvira the scrap. "These are my personal number and address. Please don't hesitate to let me know if something becomes frightening or overwhelming, or if something else that's bad happens. I would advise you not to go into the golden sphere and stick to dreaming."

She pauses before asking Alvira, "Tell me, is it tempting? The brain chip world. Do you enjoy spending time in there?"

"Why do you ask?" Alvira is cautious about how she wants to answer. *The last thing I'd want is for Dr. Dafalias to shut this thing down.*

"Your brain is a complex machine primed for solving this mathematical problem. The chip is also a different complex machine primed for solving the same mathematical problem. Together as collaborators, the two machines create a third entity entirely . . . and that must be this world you are able to enter, now a conscious communicative process. I suppose if a non-sentient machine and a sentient machine combine even partially, that combination could result in sentience like the people you described inhabiting your worlds. Truthfully, a part of me is unsure whether it would help or hurt your ability to solve the problem if you continue entering the golden portal. But the unknowns and risk to your mental state aren't worth it. I still advise against it . . . but I want to know if it's tempting."

Alvira decides to tell the truth. *Honestly, anything other than the truth would seem odd.* "Yes. It is tempting to explore the other reality. It's the stuff of my wildest imagination, turned real."

Dr. Dafalias frowns slightly, then closes the file for good. "Alright, Alvira. Keep me updated on things, you know how to reach me. We can end for this week. Thank you for telling me."

When Saturday arrives, Alvira and Kyle see Ezra and Juliani standing in the line for Enceladus along with a tall guy who must be Joe. They're talking to someone with purple hair. They wave and the two of them join their friends. Alvira hugs Juliani in greeting. She seems quiet and withdrawn today for some reason though, so Alvira gives her space.

"I think the acid's actually wearing off now," Alvira tells Kyle, and he nods. "We took a quarter tab each a while before heading over, but lost track of time." He clarifies to the rest of the group.

Ezra grins. "Kyle, Al, this is my boyfriend, Joe."

"It's so nice to meet you! At last, man." Kyle says, while Alvira smiles and waves.

"Al, Joe is a math person too." Ezra is clearly very excited about this guy.

"Oh cool! What do you study?" Alvira asks him.

"Uh, type theory." Joe says. "Just got into the math PhD program at Harvard."

Ezra leans against him. "Following in your dad's footsteps huh?"

Joe nods. "He was a Harvard alum too," he tells Alvira.

"Joe's dad wasn't just any alum either." Ezra adds. "I hear he's a real big shot in the math world."

"Really?"

Joe blushes and looks at his shoes. "My full name is Joseph Sosa."

Alvira's jaw almost drops. "Holy shit. Sosa like . . . the Fields medalist?"

"Yeah."

"Damn! You really are following in your dad's footsteps. He studied type theory too, right?" Alvira says.

"Yeah he really got me into it. We wrote this paper together when I was in high school, and it totally cemented my love for math and the idea of using type theory to describe limitations on how we perceive the world."

It's Kyle's turn to look shocked. "Bro what the fuck, you were an author on a paper in high school?"

Joe just shrugs.

"Oh!" Ezra says. "And this is a new friend we met in line. Her name's Eloisa!" He gestures to the girl standing next to them.

"I like your hair!" Alvira points to her purple curls.

"Thanks," Eloisa says. "Are you a PhD student too?"

"No, I've been trying and failing to get into a math PhD for a few years now." Alvira sighs. "I think my undergrad GPA was too low."

Eloisa shakes her head. "Fuck, that's bullshit."

Alvira nods. "Yeah, I agree. That's why I want to get in, though. As soon as I become a professor, I'd be able to make changes to the curriculum and the way people are mentored so that things actually become engaging and foster curiosity, you know?"

Eloisa looks super skeptical. "I don't think it's possible to change the thing from the inside." She takes out a pack of American Spirit cigarettes. "Do you have a lighter by any chance?"

"Well, I disagree. I think I'd be better-able to figure out how to change the system from the inside than I could from outside it, for sure . . . " Alvira takes a lighter out of her pocket and lights Eloisa's cigarette.

"That's not true at all." Eloisa laughs, almost as if to an inside joke she has with herself. "You're definitely capable of changing things from outside a system, Alvira. More than you could possibly imagine."

"Well, my plan was just—"

"Life doesn't fucking go according to plan. Ever. You think I wanted to be living at my aunt's place in my twenties? Absolutely fucking not." She holds out the pack of cigarettes to Alvira, who shrugs and takes one too but doesn't light it just yet.

When Kyle sees this, he turns to Ezra and Joe. "Wait, speaking of, did you bring . . . "

Joe nods. "I've got the coke."

"And I've got FXE," Ezra adds. "We can take turns going into that alley nearby and do a small bump of each."

Eloisa takes a puff from her cigarette. "What's FXE?"

"It's like *extra* special K. A dissociative agent like ketamine but more euphoric and stimulating. If you do too much it would be like, the ultimate K-hole though. It was apparently the party drug of the twenties." Ezra says.

Alvira's mind wanders. "I think the ultimate K-hole would be dissociating so far you enter another complete reality entirely, one that only exists in your mind." *Oh man, has the acid actually worn off?*

Kyle tells Eloisa and Joe, "Al has a brain chip that optimizes her dreams to help her make mathematical breakthroughs. She's technically not supposed to do psychedelics or dissociatives or empathogens with it, but she's doing them anyway. Now she can enter this whole other reality in her head. I tried stopping her but, well, she's her own person."

"What drugs triggered the other reality to become accessible?" Eloisa asks Alvira. "And why did you go against medical advice?"

"Um . . . well, after I did ketamine the outline of the portal that could take me to that other reality appeared, and after I did shrooms I was actually able to enter it. I went against advice precisely because I was hoping for something like what happened to happen. I'm trying to have a math breakthrough you know? One amazing enough to guarantee I get the life I want."

Kyle puts his arm around her. "You don't need drugs to have breakthroughs, Al. And you don't actually need this brain chip either. You're brilliant enough to succeed without these things."

"Thanks," Alvira says. "I agree . . . but I wish the academic establishment did too. I need to accelerate my breakthroughs to actually be competitive . . . I'm not someone with a publication from high school."

As if on cue, Joe hands her the little bags of cocaine and FXE. She tells Eloisa with a smile, "I think I'll save my American Spirit," and pockets the cigarette and her lighter.

"Too late for that, I think." Eloisa replies, and the two of them laugh.

As she walks away from the group to do the drugs, Alvira overhears Kyle say, "Juliani, you've barely said anything. What's going on with you?"

Alvira goes to the nearby alley and does a small bump of each, her mouth filling with a metallic taste from the drip. When she gets back, she hears Ezra exclaim, "You're quitting your PhD?! To work on that other sketchy brain chip project at Toabe Industries?!"

He turns to Alvira as she approaches. "No offense, with the brain chip thing."

Alvira frowns, "Uh, that wasn't offensive? And it's a totally different study?"

Juliani isn't quiet anymore. "It might be sketchy, Ezra. But at least it'll pay the fucking bills so I can actually live in this city."

Kyle is shaking his head. "We always thought you'd like, win a Nobel prize or something. Dude, you could have totally gotten a postdoc at the Affan lab."

Alvira hands the drugs to Kyle, and he heads to the alley. Juliani calls out to him, "I'm not leaving research! I'm just leaving academia!"

Ezra turns to Eloisa and Joe. "Juliani is brilliant. She switched from astroparticle theory to neuroscience, and she studies predictive processing now."

"Predictive processing, that's interesting." Joe says to her.

"Yeah, the brain can model the future way better than we thought it could. In my personal opinion, really it's almost like we're living in circular loops, following trajectories our minds have already plotted out subconsciously. The way it works reminds me of modeling light cones—the spreads of possible event trajectories an object traveling along a world line through space-time can take." Juliani responds.

"What did you study in astroparticle theory?" Eloisa asks Juliani.

"I studied the Higgs field and false vacuums—how the fabric of the universe could be completely dismantled and restructured at the subatomic levels if the Higgs boson somehow quantum tunneled to an even lower energy state than the one it's currently in." She shrugged. "It was amazing to study, so that should tell you how utterly interesting predictive processing is to have gotten me to switch fields."

"Wait, since you're a space person, I really want to know about what you think of the current McKeown administration and how they basically dismantled the 1967 Outer Space Treaty." Joe says.

Ezra says, "Technically it wasn't the McKeown administration, there was that thing where nations not in the treaty colonized a part of the moon and—"

"Come on babe, we all know the US was orchestrating that whole thing to dismantle the treaty and bring back an international space race." Joe says.

"Joe's right, the McKeown administration was definitely up to some international shenanigans with that. I mean, it kind of tracks with history, what did you expect?" Juliani adds. "You guys might not like my opinion on this one. I do like how there is now immense federal regulation on commercial exploitation of space resources . . . and while I see the point on how international competition to colonize space will likely lead to militarization of bases on the moon and Mars and heightened global tensions . . . A part of me also sees how much more of space we've explored since the treaty was dismantled. I mean, once the pressure of competition was there, we went to Venus and discovered all sorts of stuff and are now en route to a permanent base on Ganymede too!"

"Oh man, this is going to be a fun argument." Joe starts to ask Juliani more questions. Kyle returns and offers the two bags to Eloisa, but she declines.

"I'm on a half-dose of molly." She chuckles, and Kyle smiles before joining the debate about space.

"Ooh, you have molly?" Alvira asks, and Eloisa raises an eyebrow.

"Yeah, if you want some later you can find my friend. She's an older lady, like parent aged. Total Gen Z, she even has a fucking vape. You'll recognize her. Tell her 'Eloisa said you can have some.'"

Alvira smiles. "Cool, thanks." Then she asks, "Are you a PhD student, Eloisa?"

She shakes her head. "No, college wasn't for me. I wanted to go into urban planning once, but I failed out of school in my first semester. My mom had died, then I got depression, and it took a while to figure out the right antidepressants that wouldn't fuck with my ADHD meds. School was too much with all that going on, so I failed out."

Joe joins in then, saying, "Ah, fellow low GPA people!" He looks at Eloisa. "My GPA was fucked over because I was trying to adjust my anxiety meds too. Clearly it has no correlation to ability, just how stressed or unstressed you are during school." He smiles reassuringly. "But things can still work out, I mean, my GPA was abysmal, and I'm a Harvard grad student now."

Eloisa gives him a look. "Uh, you said your father is a famous mathematician who also went to Harvard?"

Joe shrugs. "I know that played a role, I was just trying to say . . . "

Eloisa sighs. "I get it, don't worry." Then she whispers to Alvira, "I'm really glad I'm on molly right now."

Alvira smiles at this. Joe rejoins the outer space debate with Juliani, Kyle, and Ezra.

"Now I spend all my time judging people I see on my day job," Eloisa says.

"Judging them? What do you mean?"

She shrugs. "It's really simple actually. You can tell a lot about a person by whether they say thank you or not. That's how I judge. I'm actually really good at remembering faces and keeping track of the people I see."

Alvira nods at this. "Fair enough! What's your day job?"

Eloisa is about to respond when she gets an alert on her touchscreen.

"Oh my god." Her face falls. "The Beast . . . it's fucking devastating." The rest of the group turns to her.

"What's the Beast?"

Eloisa gives Alvira a disappointed look, then turns to the rest of them, who are all equally clueless. "Uh, that's the name being given to the giant storm that's currently devastating the Caribbean . . . ? Aren't any of you all following the news?"

Kyle says, "Well, we've kind of been focused on the Harvard neuroscience data heist . . . "

Eloisa shakes her head. "I bet you'll care when that fucking storm changes its trajectory and heads toward all of us." She frowns. "Damn, you're a bunch of self-absorbed fucks. I was considering letting you all cut the line but . . . " She gives the group a once-over. "I think not."

Ezra frowns too. "Cut the line?"

Eloisa smirks. "At night I'm one of the DJs for this place, and the bouncer Veronica is my girlfriend." She calls out to the muscular woman at the door of the club, "Hi Ronnie!"

The bouncer blows her a kiss.

"Alright, I'm heading in." Eloisa puts out her cigarette and turns to Alvira.

"To answer your question about my day job . . . " She looks into Alvira's eyes with an indecipherable expression before walking away, and says, "I drive the motherfucking T."

Inside the club, the FXE hits, and Alvira slips into what feels like a comfortable blanket of dissociation. The booming of the music is mildly muted in her head, and the perceptual distance between her thoughts and the crowd around her grows to a much more preferable length to her than what exists in typical reality.

She keeps imagining what it would be like to have Axiom there, dancing with her. After an hour and twenty minutes of just dancing go by, still forty minutes before the FXE starts wearing off, Joe comes and finds Alvira.

"Hey . . . I'm . . . " He keeps talking, but Alvira can't hear him above the noise of the music and through the faintest hints of a K-hole-esque disconnect she has been circling for the past half hour. *Really is like extra-special K . . .* she watches the saturation of the lights around her change and dance.

Oh right. She remembers Joe.

Alvira holds her hand up to her ear, focusing on not getting distracted by the trippy visible traces of her arm's path through the air as she does so. "What . . . did . . . you say just now?"

He half-shouts in her ear. "I'M . . . SORRY for what I said about THE GPA." He steps back and swallows, then wipes sweat from his forehead before shouting in her ear again—IT WAS INSENSITIVE! I know I have privilege."

She smiles, "No worries!"

Then he continues. "I want you to know I REALLY DO CARE about MATH! And I'M GOOD AT IT too!"

Alvira frowns slightly. "Of course . . . why . . . else would you do . . . a PhD?"

Joe swallows again and looks around at the club a bit paranoid, then says, "I just don't . . . want you to think I ONLY GOT IN because of MY DAD. I WANT YOU TO KNOW I'm super PASSIONATE ABOUT math too."

"Why are you telling me all of this?" Alvira sighs. It's getting harder to dissociate, maybe the FXE is wearing off early. *This is really making me feel sober.*

Joe shrugs. "I don't know . . . " He starts mumbling again, and she can't hear him for a bit, but Alvira also much prefers holding on to the euphoria and the blurring lights.

The song ends and, in the brief pause she hears him say, "I want you to like me."

Alvira smiles at Joe again, reassuringly. "Don't worry about that, Joe. We're good. You and Ezra are really cute!" She pats his shoulder. "I'll be back, going to head to the bathroom real quick.

In the bathroom, Alvira splashes some water on her face. *Damn, maybe I am getting sober.*

She's about to leave when an older woman walks in . . . *holding a vape.*

"Are you alright?" she asks Alvira as she pockets the vape and starts washing her hands. "You look a bit stressed."

Alvira chuckles. "Yeah, I'm fine. Just hard talking to people in academia sometimes." She leans against a paper towel dispenser and feels her head spin a bit. *Hm, maybe I'm still feeling it, actually.*

The woman smiles. "Well, guess I'll be quiet then."

"You're in academia too?" Alvira looks skeptical.

The woman nods. "I'm a professor actually. I run a lab. Neuroscience. I study empathy and multi-agent systems."

"Wow . . . my boyfriend is interested in multi-agent systems too. Also, is *everyone* in Boston a fucking neuroscientist?" Alvira asks.

"I'm pretty sure that's about to change for me, actually." The woman sighs. "Everything is about to come crashing down for me."

The buzzing of the fluorescent lights is too loud.

"Is that why you're . . . uhh . . . " Alvira trails off. *Why is it so loud?*

"Yes?"

"Sorry—Is that why you're here at twenties throwback night?"

The woman laughs. "I suppose so. This was the one last thing I needed to do before the shit comes crashing down."

Alvira dries her face off with a paper towel. "If you're a neuroscience professor, how do you feel about the heist?"

She smiles. "I know of the research that was stolen quite well. Quite a feat, honestly."

"What was the research about?" Alvira asks.

The woman looks at the reflection of the two of them. "They've built an empathy machine. A type of neuroimaging that can tell you hormonal and neurochemical levels in the body in response to certain experiences and sensory stimuli and figure out the type of sensory stimuli that would instill the same physiological response in another person."

"Why would DARPA fund that?"

The woman shrugs. "It tells you how you can influence emotional and physical states of other people."

"Hmm." Alvira says, then gets to the point. "Also, do you know Eloisa?"

The woman smiles. "Yes, I do."

Alvira shrugs. "She said I could have some molly."

"Alright," the woman opens her purse. "If Eloisa said so, that is. Here is a box of half-doses." She holds out a box, and Alvira takes one of the transparent capsules filled with powder. After hesitating, the woman takes one as well.

"Are you also in academia?" she asks.

The buzzing, they've got to fix these goddamn lights. It's excruciating . . . wouldn't it like, drive away customers?

"Sorry . . . what did you say?" she asks the woman. "They've got to fix this insidious buzzing, don't you think?"

The woman looks puzzled, then shrugs it off. "I asked if you're also in academia."

Alvira sighs. "Academia-adjacent, I suppose. I work in an academic research lab as an assistant, but I don't think I'll ever make it at this point."

"Well," the woman holds up the molly pill in a *cheers* and Alvira does the same. "To the fuckery that is the academic establishment."

They swallow the pills.

The woman says, "You know, look at your reflection—high out of your mind, jaded, disillusioned . . . you're already a product of the academic establishment. My advice? Give up on those dreams, you'll have a happier life with some other career path."

Alvira frowns. "You're not very nice."

The woman laughs. "Yeah. My partner doesn't think so either."

"Something to work on?" Alvira looks at the woman, who shakes her head in response. "No, she doesn't mind me. And she is a cold, calculating woman herself. Pretty sure she would sacrifice me in an instant if it came down to choosing me or her goals for bettering the world . . . but truthfully, she makes a good leader. She can make those tough decisions. Anyway, I am rambling." The woman puts away the box of pills and smiles at Alvira. "Nice to meet you. If it had been a different time, a different place . . . I might have encouraged you instead." She shrugs before leaving the bathroom. "Goodbye."

When Alvira leaves the bathroom, she goes to find Kyle. He's talking to Ezra outside the club.

"Ezra, we've got to schmooze these PIs at COSYNE next week, so we'll get good postdocs. Agreed?"

Ezra looks worried. "I don't know how well I can schmooze though!"

Alvira walks up to them. "You guys will be fine at the neuroscience conference. You're both passionate and know what you're talking about—they'll see that."

Kyle kisses her. "Where did you go? I was starting to worry."

"Oh dude, it was bizarre. I met this older lady, she gave me molly and told me to give up on my dreams. Also I got a weird vibe that she was involved in the heist." She strokes Kyle's arm.

Kyle looks a bit concerned. "Al did you really just take molly? We're still feeling the FXE!"

She avoids the question. "I think I want to head out actually, can we go home?"

Ezra's face falls. "Aw you're leaving? Well, at least you can take the T home—it doesn't stop at midnight anymore, they changed it to run until 3 a.m. now."

"Thank fuck for that." Kyle says. "Alright Al. Let's go home."

Alvira lays in the grass next to Axiom, close to the black sphere she entered from. *It's nice that, according to Axiom, the sphere disappears soon after I leave the reality. That plus it being surrounded by trees is really helpful for keeping it hidden.*

"Have no Unveilings really occurred since I started visiting?" she asks.

"Yes, they stopped entirely." Axiom says. "So your theory about them influencing your dreams seems likely, if you have been choosing to come here instead of experiencing your dreams. Hey, Alvira," Axiom looks at her. "You were telling me about this problem you want to solve. This construction of complementary systems proving the undecidable problems of one another. I was wondering . . . isn't there a risk of creating a different system with equally valid, 'true' results, that's able to prove an undecidable problem of your original system, but also contradicts other findings of that system? If it is also expressive, and consistent . . . how do you decide what is the truth?"

Alvira smiles. "Yes, that's very true. Honestly, at least intuitively, I think there are several contradictory languages—types of math—you could use to describe the way the universe functions that would all be equally valid, too. My personal definition of objective truth is the *set* of these constructions. If you try to create new math, you have to be able to identify what element of that set the new system belongs to. It might have puzzle pieces that fit into and prove several undecidable problems from several other systems, but I think it can only *belong* to the ones where there is a constructive interference and the combination doesn't turn the whole construction into nonsense.

"I think truth is a type of invariance—and the best way to represent invariance is through the equal sign, through equality. If something is invariant, it is equal to itself. I think, at the core of each of these many valid ways to describe the universe, there will always be a thread of invariance. It might look different each time, but it will always exist, and it will always be the goal of the construction to peel apart all the things branching off that core until it is laid bare. I want to find a systematic approach to matching new mathematical systems to their complementary constructions in such a way that they'd be best able to unveil that thread of invariance. How can we identify the constructive and destructive interferences between the proofs and undecidable problems of each? That systematic approach . . . I hope it exists."

Axiom thinks about this for some time. "It reminds me of how your reality and my reality work together to uncover an answer."

Alvira feels the hint of a realization creep up, but she can't quite figure it out. "That's really accurate, actually. In my reality, we work with proofs, and," she giggles. "Theorems and lemmas and axioms."

"I still can't get over that," Axiom giggles too.

Alvira continues. "But in your reality, you work with personalities. With your intuitive desires and interpersonal structures. To solve the same thing."

Alvira's thoughts turn to Kyle, then. And Boston and her friends. *There are so many problems there, affecting everyone. Why did our species have to create so many inefficiencies in the way we answer questions about reality . . .*

"What are you thinking about?" Axiom asks.

"Multi-agent systems. It's what someone I know in my reality is interested in." *Kyle. I should think about him more . . . In here, with her, I barely think about him at all . . .*

"He thinks of a system of individuals as its own organism, with its own goals. For example, a species-wide goal is ensuring the species doesn't go extinct. But there are interspecies systems that also have other goals, and so on. Collective experiences shared by all the individuals or a significant portion of them have the power to entirely alter the structure of that multi-agent organism. For example, giving a bunch of them mind-altering substances. It changes the social structure, creates revolutions."

Oh shit. Have I been dosing this entire dodecahedron world with cocaine, acid, shrooms, molly, ketamine, and FXE? How the hell would that change the future trajectory of this place, the goal-space of all these people? Or even the past . . . time doesn't have to move linearly in a reality existing only in a brain . . . have I been changing the true history of this place? Have I been hurting these people?

Oh, fuck. Also . . .

"Axiom, something worries me about my reality and yours being complementary systems."

"What?"

"Well, they are certainly both primed for solving this mathematical problem, and there are plenty of beautiful things in both, I mean look around—" She gestures toward the trees around them.

Axiom adds, "And in yours. I still remember what you told me about the galaxies . . . "

"Yes. But there is so much corruption in my reality, so many inefficient and illogical ways the interpersonal systems are structured. There are horrific, horrific things that happen in my reality, Axiom. Even if it isn't an allocentric Earth being complementary to this dodecahedron world, even if it is my egocentric reality and my specific perceptions and thoughts collaborating with you, I am still a product of that corrupt and inefficient system and will inevitably carry pieces of it within the way I function. I'm worried that if my reality is corrupt, and if it's complementary to yours . . . there is something about your reality that will be really corrupt too. Not just unfairness in how people Unveil, but something truly, incomprehensibly horrific."

Axiom stays quiet for a long time. "Well, I definitely don't want to think about that." she eventually says. "Speaking of mind-altering substances . . . have you tried portal wine yet?" She holds up her bag of portal wine with a wicked grin.

"No, but I have been dying to try that shit." Alvira grins back. "What fucking drugs has my mind invented?!"

The portal wine tastes sweet and milky. Pretty soon after drinking it, Alvira looks around in awe. The fractal shapes in the plants and structure of the world seem to warp into continuously doubling rotational symmetries. And when she looks around, she can see countless ghostly, translucent, alternative versions of herself and Axiom in the surroundings, some with Lemma there too, some without, some with a tall woman wearing a long transparent cloak, some where she is alone . . . and as far as the eye can see. She is certain there would be more seen on the other Faces, too.

"The wine allows you to witness other potential trajectories within Truth's goal-space." Axiom looks at Alvira and seems surprised. "Alvira, look at your—oh, never mind."

"What?"

"For a moment, I thought I saw markings flowing across your skin. But it must have been a hallucination."

Alvira looks around. "It's my light cone in this place."

Axiom looks puzzled, so Alvira clarifies. "My friend Juliani—you would love her if the two of you were able to meet—once studied astroparticle theory, a way to study our Universe. She told me about light cones, the spread of future trajectories through space-time an object could take given its current position within it."

She goes up to the black sphere that leads into the Belly. *There are no alternative versions of you, in this place, though. Your position is the same in every trajectory . . . you are an invariant.* She mentally tells the sphere and reaches out to touch its boundary. *Woah.*

"Axiom, are you seeing this?"

Axiom nods in awe.

Alvira finds she is able to change the size of the sphere while under the influence of portal wine. She and Axiom laugh as she expands the thing to a giant, then shrinks it down to fit in the palm of her hand, before returning it to its original size.

"I wonder what that's about." she says as she falls back onto the floor next to Axiom, surrounded by countless versions of them also falling onto the floor, some versions superimposed onto their own bodies.

Axiom is looking into Alvira's eyes, and Alvira turns serious when she sees the expression on Axiom's face.

"You are the first person I've met who fully understands me." Axiom says and holds Alvira's hand.

Some of the alternative versions of the two of them begin to lean into each other.

Some of the alternative versions of the two of them kiss.

Alvira studies these futures, these myriad choices, trajectories, and paths she could take displayed around her. She sees Axiom doing the same.

"When I'm with you, I forget about the disappointments and frustrations in the world I'm from." Alvira tells Axiom. "There is nothing but pure wonder, and curiosity, and discovery." They draw closer together. "You . . . you don't know how lucky I am to have met you."

Axiom puts her hand on Alvira's stomach, and Alvira continues.

"When I'm with you, I don't want to go back, Axiom. I want to stay."

Axiom touches the side of Alvira's face. "Then stay," she says, before their lips meet.

This feels right, Alvira thinks as she kisses Axiom, as the countless ghostly versions of them go about their various life paths around her. *This is beautiful,* she thinks as they remove their iridescent cloaks.

Later, when the effects of the portal wine have worn off and the ghostly alternatives have disappeared, the two of them lay out of breath on a pile of their clothes on the forest floor, taking comfort in the warmth of each other's skin, Alvira tucks a strand of Axiom's hair behind her ear, then starts putting on her clothes. "I can't stay, though."

"I know," Axiom smiles a bit sadly. "I'm happy for the times you can visit us here. But you have your reality too. With your galaxies."

Alvira thinks about this. "You know, it's unfair that I get to see both realities, and you only get to see one. You deserve to see images of a galaxy, Axiom. You deserve to see Boston, meet Juliani, eat our food . . . you deserve to see the Universe you live in, too."

Axiom laughs a bit. "But how?"

Alvira smiles and takes her hand. "Come back through the sphere with me! Or go instead of me! You can inhabit my body and experience whatever you want to experience, learn whatever you want to learn. I have a feeling you will be just as astounded as I was to have seen this place. Come on!"

Alvira stands and starts entering the sphere, keeping her head and arm outstretched to Axiom.

"Are you sure?" Axiom seems nervous, and Alvira grins with confidence. "I'm sure, come on, we've got to at least try it!"

After a moment of hesitation, Axiom grins too. "Okay." She takes Alvira's hand, and Alvira pulls her arm into the sphere.

Wait, what's wrong? I'm not holding her arm any more . . . Alvira, in the Belly, holds nothing but empty space. She quickly puts her head into the golden sphere again before it disappears and sees Axiom crying on the forest floor. Her arm is gone, ending just below her shoulder in a blurred, shadowy stump.

"Axiom, I didn't know! I . . . I didn't know! I thought . . . "

Axiom looks at Alvira with a look of hurt, anger, and disappointment that shakes Alvira to her core.

"Just go." Axiom says in a low voice. "Leave this place, and *never* come back."

Alvira wakes up sobbing. Kyle is shaking her, looking really concerned.

"Al, holy shit, I was worried!" he says.

"What?" she says through tears.

Kyle frowns. "Al, you've been asleep for over fourteen hours. It was impossible to wake you up. Dude, look." He holds his touchscreen to her face.

Alvira wipes away her tears. "That's impossible, I was only in there for less than a day, barely any time should have passed here." Then she looks at his touchscreen, showing a news article headline, reading:

Professor Octavia Setzer Arrested for Suspected Involvement in Harvard Neuroscience Data Heist.

"Al, she was *on my dissertation committee.* This can't be happening now, I'm leaving for COSYNE in a few days!"

Alvira studies the image of the woman in the article. "Kyle, this was the lady who gave me molly at Enceladus last night . . . I swear."

"What? There is *no* way." Kyle looks frightened. "Are you sure?"

Alvira nods.

"What the fuck." Kyle puts his head in his hands. "What the actual fuck." Then he looks at her. "Wait, why were you crying when you woke up? Are you okay?"

She leans into him and starts crying again. "Kyle I did something bad. I did something really bad. I cheated . . . "

Kyle pulls away, and tears start to fill his eyes too. "What? What do you mean? When . . . "

"When I was in the dodecahedron world, with this woman named Axiom . . . "

Kyle breathes a sigh of relief, but his expression turns from hurt to worried. "You cheated on me . . . with a figment of your imagination?"

"She's *real* Kyle. All of them are. That reality is just as valid as this one! And I hurt her too, oh god . . . "

Kyle pulls Alvira close. "Al, I know you wanted me to give you space on this one, but . . . can you maybe go easy on the drugs while you have this brain chip? I am seriously worried about you right now."

Alvira nods. "I agree. I'm going to stop with the drugs for a bit." She buries her head into his T-shirt. "And I'm never going back into that other reality again."

That night, when Alvira is in the Belly, she chooses the silver sphere, entering a dream.

==

As soon as Unveilings started again, I convinced Contradiction to assign me and Lemma as the iridescent cloaks in charge of an upcoming one. I was fitted with a prosthetic arm, though I often keep it removed and trace the strange blurriness of the stump my arm ends in now.

I was blind with attraction, with awe. Not anymore. My resentment toward Alvira, the creator, has only grown. What happened that day made me rethink everything.

"It's not beautiful for our entire life purposes to be molded to fit this woman's desire to solve a mathematical problem. It's a fucked up deterministic prison, and I want to break out." I told Lemma, and after hearing me out, hearing my plan, she agreed.

There was one useful piece of advice Alvira gave me. At the next Unveiling, I plan to grab onto the chosen as they enter Truth and see what the Thirteenth Face really is. And see if I can break it.

The next person to be chosen is a very old woman. She directs her luminescence into the groove of the Mountain Temple's door, it opens, and she, Lemma, and I enter. My palms sweat, my heartbeat pounds in my head deafeningly.

We enter the topmost chamber, housing our god. I stare into the infinitely complex fractal structure of the Mandelbrot set, waiting to take charge of my own destiny.

The woman's luminescence is pulled toward one of the embedded Julia sets, the miniature cardioid at its center expands, and the woman begins to be absorbed into it. When only her head remains, in a monotonous mechanical voice, she says:

"INFINITE GARBLE EXTENSION"

I grab onto the woman's head, and Lemma grabs onto me.

"What are you—"

"I'm coming with you, Axiom." Lemma says. "Always."

We are absorbed into Truth.

It is dark for a while as our eyes adjust.

Then, we look around.

"We're in the center of the world." Lemma says.

We are standing on a floating pentagonal platform. The miniature dodecahedral temples surround us, with the exception of the Mountain Temple.

The old woman who was chosen is wrapped in light, almost seeming swaddled in it, entirely immobile. She does not react to anything, she is hypnotized.

"What are you doing here?!" Contradiction climbs from a ladder onto the platform. "You're not supposed to—it's dangerous here! The two of you need to LEAVE—"

She is cut short by a rumbling sound, one that grows louder and louder.

"Oh no," Contradiction says. "The Beast of Dreams."

The fragments of light providing the scraps of perceptible sight we were holding onto start to amalgamate, spinning and spinning into a massive whirlwind of illumination, a vast storm of light taking up the entire space around us, the eye of the storm directly centered on us. When I look into the thing, I realize it's not a disk at all but a tunnel, and then I notice teeth within the eye of the storm, serrated things lining an infinitely long digestive tract.

"GET DOWN!" Contradiction pulls me and Lemma to the floor of the platform. The Beast of Dreams lifts the chosen old woman up into the air and swallows her whole. It starts to shrink, then, thankfully, as Contradiction, Lemma, and I cling to the floor of the platform.

Lemma lets out a whimper, and when I look at her, my heart drops. The storm is shrinking, but it is now centered directly above her, just barely above the top of her head.

Almost as though it is studying her. I think, as the Beast of Dreams finally dissipates entirely.

We stopped being priests that day. Contradiction revealed to us the nature of our true god, the Beast of Dreams, a creature that digests each of us in a process that converts us to a dream and feeds the reality to the creator of the world. This is what the door at the bottom of each temple leads to, that the transparent-cloaked priests guard. Lemma and I did not tell her we met the creator.

The transparent cloaks knew about Alvira, knew the nature of the reality, how each citizen of the world was destined to die and become a dream.

"During a dream, you are able to show the creator whatever you want to show." Contradiction said. "And you saw the woman, the feeding process is painless, her mind was entirely dissociated."

"How could you?" we asked her. "How could you let something like that happen?"

Contradiction only sighed and said something about how our anger was exactly a reminder of why the ranks of priesthood were important, how the information would only make sense when delivered slowly through the ranks of the white and transparent cloaks above us.

"Unfortunately, you will not get that opportunity, Lemma and Axiom. With this, your priesthood is being revoked." she told us sadly.

When we went home that day, resentment at the structure and manipulative nature of the world burned in our guts.

"We spent all our lives dreaming of being transparent cloaks." Lemma shook her head.

"Yet it feels freeing to leave all of that behind." I told her, and she agreed.

The next time someone is chosen for an Unveiling, it confirmed the feeling of dread that had gripped my heart ever since that day. A part of me knew it was coming.

The next person to be chosen is Lemma.

I walk with her all the way to the Mountain Temple, even though I am not allowed to enter it. Both of us are crying. Everything seems to move too fast, her luminescence opening the door, the ramp extending for her to enter. Before she enters the temple, Lemma with her blinding luminescence embraces me, and says:

"I will convince her to return here, with my dream. Convince her to stay in this reality forever. So that the Beast of Dreams will never kill one of us, ever again. Go wait for her on Face Five. I love you, Axiom."

==

In Alvira's dream, she soon realizes she is inhabiting Lemma. She zooms through the dodecahedron world, sees Lemma's parents, her childhood, grows up in the little wooden house. She sees Axiom and feels both her own desire and ache to hold and kiss her again, along with Lemma's deep platonic care.

Then, she sees Unveilings. Over and over again, people being illuminated by a blinding light and entering the Mountain Temple. She sees Lemma's parents Unveil, she sees children Unveil, elderly people, young people, all sorts of people, entering into the massive floating dodecahedron of the Mountain Temple.

She enters the temple herself, with Axiom and an old woman who has been chosen. She grabs onto Axiom as Axiom grabs onto the woman and enters through the Mandelbrot portal.

She sees the Beast of Dreams. Feels the pain, the fear, the rewriting of pleasant memories as horrific ones.

She sees her own skin illuminated when she becomes chosen, feels the compulsion to move to the Mountain Temple, how the world goes dark right as she enters the Mandelbrot portal.

Then she is taken to a memory of Lemma, Alvira, and Axiom sitting around a table at Lemma's house.

"It's true," she hears Axiom say.

"When you're in this reality with us, Alvira, all Unveilings cease."

Alvira spends the next day calmly walking around Boston. Kyle left for COSYNE the previous day. She eats at her favorite restaurants and gets a crispy chicken sandwich from the McDonald's at Kenmore. She walks for a while in the Commons, then goes to read in the public library. Finally, Alvira takes the T to Seaport and sits on the outdoor wooden steps of the Institute of Contemporary Art, looking out over the ocean as the sky grows darker and darker.

She looks through the news alerts on her touchscreen. About how that massive storm is heading toward the Northeast . . . and another headline, reading:

Professor Octavia Setzer Found Dead in Prison.

She sighs, then sends Kyle a simple message.

I'm sorry Kyle, but I'm leaving. I can contribute a lot more to that other reality than I can contribute to this one. Thank you for everything. I love you.

She turns off her touchscreen.

Before she lies down on the ICA steps and lets the sound of the waves lull her to sleep, Alvira takes out the cigarette Eloisa gave her and smokes it all.

"I know what to do," Alvira says as she enters the dodecahedron world, Axiom waiting there in front of the black sphere. "Give me portal wine, please, before I change my mind."

"You're lucky I stole some from the temple before my priesthood was revoked." Axiom says and hands her a bag of wine. Alvira drinks from it deeply.

When she can see all the alternative versions of herself, she begins to cry. So many of them are returning through the portal, going back to Boston, to Kyle, to that world and life she really does care about so much. But she steels herself and approaches the portal.

Alvira takes hold of the portal and makes it smaller and smaller and smaller, until it is in the palms of her hands again. With a final pressure and a final burst of resolve, Alvira squeezes the sphere out of existence.

As soon as she does so, she looks down at her arms and notices geometric patterns of light flowing over her skin.

Then she hears someone cry out from a nearby tree. Contradiction steps out into the clearing.

"I don't have the markings of Truth anymore!" she exclaims, and it's true. She is no longer marked, there are no patterns of light flowing over the priest woman's skin.

"Were you following me?" Axiom asks her, and Contradiction avoids her gaze.

When Alvira closed the opening in the boundary between their realities for good, everyone in the dodecahedron world lost the markings for an Unveiling . . . while Alvira gained them.

As the decades passed within the reality, Alvira kept waiting for The Beast of Dreams to choose her. But she didn't live an unfulfilling life as she waited. She explored, studied, helped Axiom dismantle the priesthood and create a council of education in its place that combined methods of study from both the realities, without any of the corruption.

She and Axiom never fell in love again, but after years they did once again become friends.

On the hundredth anniversary of Alvira closing the boundary between worlds, when Alvira is an ancient woman, she is finally chosen by the Beast of Dreams.

"I'm not afraid," she tells Axiom before she enters the Mountain Temple. "In some ways, I have been waiting for this moment for most of my life."

Alvira enters the Mountain Temple alone, climbs up the pentagonal spiral of a ramp in the hollow dodecahedral pyrite crystal, toward her destiny.

When she approaches the Mandelbrot portal, it begins to zoom, but not into any embedded Julia. It zooms into a spot far from the set, not contained within it.

Alvira's last thought before the world goes dark isn't a word.

It is a laugh.

==

Lisa Dafalias stands in the empty T station, smoking one of her niece's cigarettes. The place was deemed a flooding risk with the upcoming storm and was evacuated entirely. It's the perfect place for her group to meet.

She takes out a small photograph of Octavia and sets fire to it with the cigarette.

I'm sorry, my love, she thinks. *But what the dead mathematician told me was right . . . You were getting careless, a liability to the mission. I had to take care of the liability. You were a key, and I had to throw away the key . . . Yours was a necessary death, Octavia.*

"Auntie Lisa, are you coming to this meeting or not?" Eloisa pokes her head out of a T maintenance room. "It's a pretty big risk to all be meeting, you know? Ronnie messed with the security camera footage, but still."

Lisa nods, puts out the cigarette, and discards the burned photograph.

In the meeting room, she stands while the others sit.

"This is our final meeting, you all. With what happened to Octavia, it is too risky to meet any longer. The goals of our mission have been met . . . It has been a time of major wins and major losses, hasn't it." She looks around at them. "We are all feeling the loss of Octavia, she was such a core part of this mission, she helped with so much. And . . . I loved her." Lisa keeps her eyes open long enough for a tear to form, then wipes it away.

"And nobody wanted the young mathematician Alvira to die. We were only trying to get information about interactions between the brain chip and mind-altering substances that would allow us to come up with enough harmful hypotheses to end the DARPA-funded Toabe Industries brain chip study. Thanks to Octavia and her role in stealing the neuroimaging data from the Harvard lab, we know that the project would have used the lab's findings to influence the programming of that brain chip and consequently the participants' thoughts and emotions."

I really didn't want Alvira to die. Hers was an unnecessary death. I felt for her, I wanted her to solve her mathematical problem. But there is a small silver lining to the whole situation.

"But, with the death of the young mathematician and knowledge being made public about her usage of mind-altering substances while she had the Mimpi chip, the DARPA-funded Toabe Industries brain chip-mind-altering substance project has been shut down! That was the ultimate goal, and might I say, a small silver lining."

Someone stands up abruptly, and Eloisa gives the person a look. "Dr. Banks, wait for Auntie Lisa to finish speaking!"

"It's okay, Eloisa." Lisa smiles at her niece then turns to the woman standing up. "What is it, Cynthia?"

Cynthia shakes her head. "I'm out, Lisa. This was too much. I was all for shutting down that creepy McKeown administration DARPA military project, but two people *died* because of what we did." She looks at Eloisa. "You were on the fence about Alvira, about the plan to give her molly at Enceladus, remember? Then you changed your mind all of a sudden! You were the last vote, you could have shut the whole thing down."

Eloisa shrugs. "She didn't say thank you to me when she got off the T."

Cynthia scoffs as she walks out, and says to Lisa before leaving, "You are walking down a dark path, Lisa. You can't burn down these systems just to build other corrupt ones in their place."

After the meeting, Lisa packs her belongings to head to the storm shelter that's been set up. Eloisa has already headed over there. Suddenly, she hears an angry banging at the front door.

Lisa opens the door to find Alvira's boyfriend Kyle, tears streaming down his face, holding up the slip of paper she had given Alvira with her home address written on it.

"I heard you were with her when she died!" he says, in almost a shout.

Lisa invites him in and makes tea for the two of them.

"Yes, when she was in her coma, I visited her." she says to the young man. "And yes, on one of those visits, she woke up briefly, and then died." *The expression on her face still haunts me . . .*

Kyle wipes away his tears and takes a sip of tea. "I can't believe she's gone. They're waiting to do her funeral until after the storm. Those news headlines got everything wrong about her. Her lifestyle, her personality, everything. She was . . . she was *brilliant.* She deserved a bright future."

"Well, in some ways a part of her is still alive." Lisa tries to comfort him. "That chip, in the autopsy, never turned off. Whatever was in there is still running."

This doesn't seem to comfort him much. Lisa sips her tea with him in silence for a while.

Eventually, Kyle asks her, "Did she say anything before she died? When she woke up, briefly. Did she say anything to you?"

"Yes. She said," Lisa hesitates.

I will never forget the way she looked at me. Euphoric, with the wisdom of a hundred year old woman in her expression. Tears of joy running down her face, grinning ear to ear, she looked at me and simply said, "'I solved it.'"

==

When Alvira underwent the final Unveiling, the world changed. It turned slow, the vibrancy and detail of it left the place. The oceans lost their waves, the desert sands lost their sparkle, the cities would only appear in a spot directly in front of your vision.

I went to the center of the world again, one day. The Beast of Dreams has disappeared, seeming to have exploded into many small dodecahedral pyrite crystals now lining the place.

I don't know how slow the processing speed of the chip we live on has become, the scholars just calculated it slowed. Perhaps one thought will take me eons now. It is bittersweet, the idea of my mind matching the cosmic scale of galaxies in a Universe I will never truly be able to see.

But I don't mind inhabiting this wire frame world, even if it has lost much of its former beauty. All of us can now carve our own destinies, our desires are no longer held prisoner to a different reality.

We are now free.

ABOUT THE AUTHOR

Arula Ratnakar is a neuroscientist and hard science fiction author. Her short science fiction can be found in *Clarkesworld Magazine* and the *Life Beyond Us* anthology. She works in a lab where she researches the neural mechanisms of psychedelics and dissociative agents.

The People from the Dead Whale

DJUNA, TRANSLATED BY JIHYUN PARK AND GORD SELLAR

1.

The whale sat about ten kilometers away from our raft.

Looking through the binoculars I got from Mum, I saw the white foam that surrounded its huge black body as it moved against the current, and a red flag flying from a pole planted in its back. As I peered more closely, I could've sworn I could see buildings there, and fishing boats all around the whale. Believing my eyes was risky, but given our circumstances, I was ready to believe anything.

A light rain began to fall. I got back under our waterproof tarpaulin and took my paddle back up. We had to keep rowing constantly in order to avoid being swept toward Day or Night. I found myself missing our old whale, which had kept us safe by swimming against the current. Still, ultimately, everything comes to an end. Our tribe had lived there for twelve hundred years, or about forty Earth years. Whether the whale had contracted some disease or just come to the end of its life cycle, we couldn't know, except that we'd done nothing wrong . . . it just turned out that we'd somehow chosen a whale with only twelve hundred years left to live.

A yellow signal flame lit up from the side of a distant whale: they'd sighted us too.

After quite a long wait, I saw a little dinghy approaching. There was a pair of people in white hazmat suits seated inside it. As they got closer, I heard the faint *tunk-tunk* rhythm of an air compressor motor spewing out water. The motor slowed as they got near us, but they never cut it completely.

One of the pair called out to us with a masculine voice, "You're from the Sunflower Whale?"

"That's right," Mum replied. "There's twenty-one of us, and we're . . ."

She was cut off immediately: "Don't get any closer to us than that."

"We're clean," my mum said. "We haven't lost anyone for almost for a year."

That second part was a lie. Two people had killed themselves, and one had drowned accidentally. Still, it was true that nobody had died from *sickness*. Considering that that's what they were really interested in, Mum wasn't *really* lying. It's not like there was any point in telling them our whole life story and prolonging this situation any more than we had to.

The one with the masculine voice said, "We've got no reason to believe anything you say."

"In that case, how about you letting us stay within a certain range, closer to you?" my mum replied. "Say, a kilometer away. You can take your time and verify what I'm saying. We're all exhausted, and we can't keep on constantly rowing our boat forever . . ."

As the conversation went on, she seemed to persuade the people on the boat, though you might not have thought so by the sound of their voices.

Finally, the boat disappeared again toward the whale, its motor still *tunk-tunking*. Rowing on constantly, we gazed across the foggy current that began to flow, forming a barrier between the whale and our raft.

Three hours later, the dinghy returned. This time, it carried an additional person, a figure dressed not in a hazmat suit like the other two, but instead in a gray frock of woven seaweed. The figure was beardless, which made them look like a woman, and carried on their back an enormous bundle bound in place with a white cloth.

When they reached about twenty meters from our raft, the pair in the hazmat suits shoved this third person with the bundle off the boat and into the water. The person with the bundle didn't seem surprised by this and just started swimming toward us. Pulling the swimmer up onto our raft, we discovered a long rope had been tied around their waist, tethering them back to the dinghy. Our new passenger slipped the rope loose and then tied it to our raft's broken mast. A few moments passed, and then the rope pulled taut and the dinghy started towing us behind it. We hesitated for a moment, until Mum gave us the signal, and we all stopped rowing.

At that point, our new passenger reached into their bundle and pulled out fruit, handing it to us one by one.

I wept. It was my first taste of fruit in two years.

2

We'd tried our best to keep our whale, Sunflower, alive. We'd put together all the knowledge and experience that we'd collectively accumulated in our three thousand years on this tidally locked world, but it hadn't been enough. A century of Earth time isn't really that short, but we lacked the tools and materials necessary to get anything meaningful done.

For us, this was an ocean planet. Not that it lacked continents, but the continents it had were just of no use to us: Day was a desert of sand, while Night was a desert of ice. The only place on this world where life could survive was in the twilight oceans of the terminator zone between the two. Somewhere on those continents, there likely had to be some useful resources like metals, which we could've used to establish a civilization on this world . . . but that was as helpful to us as a picture of food to a starving person. We'd searched high and low for three thousand years to find a single island on which to found a civilization, and in the end it'd all been for nothing.

The whales had been our only alternative. Now, "whales" was what we called them, but these creatures were nothing like the whales back on Earth. This world's whales were like enormous islands, between one and two hundred meters wide and stretching from seven hundred to fifteen hundred meters long. As they swam with hundreds of fins beneath the waves, their flat backs stayed steady above the waterline.

A few thousand years' observation had led us to the conclusion that they were actually made up of hundreds of individual creatures living in symbiosis, though the relationships they shared were much more complicated than any symbiotic colony back on Earth. Evolutionarily, bulking up had proved to be a solid path to survival in this harsh environment where, if you were swept in the wrong direction by rough currents or a typhoon, a fish could in a single instant end up being a steamed or frozen solid.

On a whale's back, our survival had seemed possible. We'd been able to build homes, plant farms within reach of the sea, and peel off skin from their backs to use for building ourselves boats. We'd been able to bear children and educate them and keep alive the dream of communicating with other stars someday. For three thousand years, that hope had kept us going.

Now, everything depended on the continued survival of the whales. Everyone had thought that whales might live forever, since as older members died from old age, there were always younger individuals ready to take their place while in the whale colony. There was a loose network of nerves that seemed to preserve and share the memories of older individuals after they died, so the whale had always appeared to continue being the same creature that we'd always known.

But then some of the whales began to die. When the mortality rate among the individuals in a given colony grew too high for reproduction to keep pace, whales died. Once the rate of death within a colony passed a certain point, external individuals sensed a crisis within the colony and stopped approaching and joining them. Then the whales became to fall apart, with the villages built on their backs collapsing along with them.

It was a "whale disease," people said. It was "contagious," they claimed. Word spread that when one whale died, the others nearby also began to die off, too. Epidemiologically, we knew nothing about if or how the condition actually spread: the infection could have traveled via oceanic currents, or through the fish they consumed . . . or even from us. One reason why we were able to adapt to life within this planet's ecosystem without specialized equipment was because of how similar this world's biosphere was to Earth's. We could eat the kinds of things that lived here, and they could eat things from our world; we could be infected by this world's microbes, and this world had somehow taken in the microbes from Earth too. For a long time, this hadn't led to anything significant.

Not until the whale disease had begun to spread. Not until other whales began dying, one by one, when their communities had taken in refugees from the first dying whales.

We resented those people, but we couldn't blame them. In their shoes, we'd have done the same thing.

3.

The woman who came from the Rose Whale was a doctor.

She was also a murderer: "I killed my husband," she told us calmly.

We didn't ask why. She must have had her reasons, just as the people who'd sent her, a murderer, to us surely had their reasons for doing so. Things get complicated when you have to deal with criminals: executing them would mean constantly reducing the number of hands on deck, but there weren't enough big whales around anymore for us to build a prison or something. You could see the logic in just wanting to make it someone else's problem: send the complications this murderer created over to the raft full of people who might, after all, be contagious carriers for the whale disease anyway. Losing a doctor this way must have been slightly unfortunate for them. Then again, if they were willing to send her to us, perhaps they had another doctor on board, too.

She examined us one by one, but she couldn't do it as thoroughly as people on other worlds: we'd used up so much of the medical supplies we'd carried on the ship that had brought us here, and the needles and syringes that were left were almost three thousand years old. Most people didn't survive much past fifty Earth years.

After she finished with the examinations, Mum asked her, "So, what do you think?"

"To be honest, I don't know," replied the doctor. "You all look healthy. Nobody has the rash, and nobody's running a fever, but we don't know anything about this whale plague. People see a fever and heat rash and panic about whale infection, but for all we know whatever's killing them might not even be transmitted by people at all. Or people could be totally asymptomatic carriers. All the rules everyone's following now . . . they're pretty close to pure superstition."

"So what do you think those people over there are going to do?"

"Well, they might let you in after a quarantine period, once they get tired of waiting. Maybe a local year . . . no more than a few Earthweeks at most."

Mum squatted down and fished her pocket watch out from her pocket. That ticking device still showed the date and time of her city back on our home world, thousands of lightyears away. Like most sensible folks, Mum cursed our ancestors who'd left the Earth and decided to pioneer their way to new planets. She was tortured by nostalgia for a home world she'd only ever seen in a few photographs: London, Taipei, New York, Nairobi, Sydney, and Rio de Janeiro. A world of enormous terrain and countless buildings. A place where Day and Night weren't the names of places.

"We thought about giving up and letting ourselves drift on the currents. I mean, what's the point of a life without hope? If I didn't have a daughter, I probably would really have done it, too. The rest of us are almost all over forty: how much longer could we really survive out there, anyway? And what would be the point, even if we could do it?"

"It's painful to just give up and die."

"Steamed to death or frozen solid. Which one would you choose?"

This was a question we'd all have heard plenty of times, like everyone on this world. This was one of the most important ways of categorizing people, often more important even than a person's gender. The doctor didn't reply, but we got the sense she was probably one of the freezers.

Mum sighed and slipped the watch back into her pocket.

"It's not so bad as all that, now. At least we don't need to paddle the raft to stay alive. We're all so exhausted."

4.

One year passed, and then two, but the inhabitants of the Rose Whale didn't take us in. Occasionally one or two of them rode that boat over toward us for a talk, but that was it. Our lack of red pox markings did nothing to convince them that we were safe.

Still, those two years were bearable. We no longer had to paddle constantly, and the Rose Whale guided us along the calm byways between the endless storms. Everywhere the inhabited whales went, an abundant ecosystem followed, so we were able to fill our bellies just by fishing and gathering food. Although we lost one of our freshwater distillation units, we were able to build a new one out of skin shed by the Rose Whale.

What worried us was the towline that tethered us to the Rose Whale. The production of strong, durable rope was among the most prized of the techniques we'd developed over the past three millennia, but no rope lasts forever. The Rose Whale people didn't even seem to give the slightest thought to swapping in a new rope. Maybe they just had hoped that the rope might get severed somehow, so they could be rid of us without having to feel guilty about it.

One day, a little more than two years after we'd first gotten tethered to the Rose Whale, the doctor discovered another whale. It was smaller than Rose or Sunflower, our old whale, only about six hundred meters long. When we looked at it through our binoculars, we could see fragments of some ramshackle buildings, but nobody moving around. That whale's back contained nothing but a ruin. For whatever unknown reason, whoever had lived there had abandoned it before even finishing construction of their village.

We watched people from the Rose Whale, in hazmat suits, board their boat and ride out on a scouting mission to the new whale. We saw them climb up onto its back and go to explore the abandoned village there. We also put our heads together and discussed it: that whale still didn't belong to anyone yet. If the Rose Whale people wouldn't accept us, maybe we could go there?

That might sound like a simple solution to our problem, but it wasn't. The Rose Whale people might want to send some of their own people to live on that whale. Whale villages were always a bit crowded, so there were always young people eager to leave their home whale. Since they thought we might be whale disease carriers, wouldn't they have a problem sharing a whale with us?

"What's the point of hesitating?" said the carpenter, the oldest person on our raft. "Those Rose Whale folks don't like towing us around anyway. Why not just go over there and set ourselves up all over the place? As soon as they see that we're there, they'll just declare the whale contaminated . . . and if any of them is willing to move there anyway, just let 'em join us."

I was frightened, but everyone else, including Mum, all agreed. Well, except the doctor, who didn't exactly agree or disagree. She kind of seemed to feel like she wasn't really one of us yet. Still, when it came time to sit and paddle, she sat down right alongside us and joined in. The towline that had constantly remained taut until a moment earlier suddenly came loose and sank into the sea.

According to Mum's watch, we arrived at the new whale after about an hour of paddling. As we approached, we found an intact dock still attached to the whale's left flank. We realized that the people who'd lived here before hadn't departed after abandoning their rough construction project after all: the buildings had been ripped apart by storms.

We all climbed up onto the whale. There wasn't much left intact, but for us even a few buildings in good condition would have been plenty. We could slowly collect lumber from sea trees to build more houses. Still, it was bizarre that the former inhabitants of the whale had departed, abandoning a village in decent condition like this.

While searching around the village, we ran into the Rose Whale people in their hazmat suits. They didn't really seem very surprised to see us.

The person who was apparently their leader said, "The houses appear to have been destroyed relatively recently. It seems like the whale's swum through a number of very harsh storms lately."

That in itself wasn't strange. Whales *try* to avoid rough weather as much as possible, and they're good at it, but this world is filled with storms. Extreme convection currents develop when hot air from Day and cold air from Night meet in the twilight zone where we live. No matter how smart or experienced a whale might be, it can't avoid storms completely. Still, most villages were built to withstand such weather: houses were built in aerodynamic shapes to reduce wind damage, and they were strongly anchored to whale's backs to avoid collapse from shock or strain. That said, since most of this village's buildings had been flung away by a recent storm—could all of the people who'd lived here simply have suffered the same fate, too?

The Rose Whalers in their hazmat suits prepared to retreat. The new whale *looked* good. But now was the time for caution. It was better, they knew, to stay in their own, familiar village until the mysterious whale plague subsided. That made sense to me, and it also came as a relief. We still had all of our hopes riding on this whale.

Sadly, our hope evaporated a few minutes later.

As the Rose Whalers started making their way toward the dock where they'd tied up their boat, I felt the first tremor. At first, I thought it probably was no big deal. We'd lived on the back of a living creature before, and it's natural for animals to move around. But when the second tremor came, there was something *very* different about it.

The whale was coming apart. Everywhere except around the docks, the "shore" of the whale was collapsing at terrifying speed. Now we could see that more than half of the symbiotic individuals making up the outer fringe of the whale's body were already dead. Usually, whales sloughed off dead individuals, but on this whale, somehow the living ones had continued clinging to the dead.

Then, suddenly, half of the surface area of the whale just instantly collapsed away, sending us scrambling for the middle of the whale's back. Two of the white-suited Rose Whalers screamed as they tumbled into the water, which was now clouded with blood. Living individuals of the whale's symbiotic body were attacking the people in the water. We'd gotten so used to how, in their peaceful symbiotic state, they lived off plankton and sea bugs; we'd forgotten about how prior to symbiotic merging, the individuals that composed them were predatory creatures. It had been unknown why, even after their merging, individuals had retained their predatory instincts and their fangs.

As all this happened, the whale also began to shift course. We knew then that we had to choose: would we stay on the whale or return to our raft?

We chose the raft. Even if we couldn't understand what was happening, we could see that this whale was not going to accept becoming our new home.

The dock hadn't yet collapsed, and the raft remained intact, too. Individuals approached us with fangs bared, but there was nothing we could do about them. One by one, our people leaped into the raft and seized the paddles.

But as I was about to run for the boat, my left foot got stuck in a hole that had opened down into the collapsing whale's body. My ankle got caught in the sticky goop that bonded individuals together, and I couldn't pull myself free.

The first person to run over to me was the doctor. The next was Mum, our village's leader. Nobody else followed them—no, nobody else *could* follow them. The people on the raft got shoved away from the whale in an instant, a few of them tumbling into the water and the rest of them holding up their paddles and fighting off the symbiotes.

That was the last of them that I ever saw.

By the time Mum and the doctor had just barely managed to free my ankle from the sticky goo, the whale was hurling itself straight into a storm as if it had completely lost its mind.

5.

We survived. The whale eventually disappeared into the storm, seemingly intent on killing us. However, the last wooden house left standing on its back had been solidly constructed and was strong enough to stand up to this desperate struggle. Luckily for us, the house had ended up in the water and now floated like a little boat, shielding us from the tempest.

Still, it was a hopeless situation. With neither paddle nor sail, floating adrift like this, it was inevitable that a current would eventually sweep us off toward Day or Night. Only death awaited us.

What had just happened? We thought it over, but as far as we knew, nobody had ever experienced or witnessed anything like this. Still, three thousand years is far too short a time to have seen everything. Perhaps the reason we didn't know about this phenomenon was because nobody who'd experienced it before had survived.

"Maybe, to the whales, *we're* the disease," said the doctor. "We tried to see our symbiosis with them in the most positive way possible, because we couldn't survive without them," she explained. "But *they* didn't need *us*. To them, we were nothing more than just bearable pests. What happens if some bearable pest starts infecting them with a deadly disease? Don't the whales need to respond to that kind of situation? They're very intelligent: they can track ocean currents, predict storms, and communicate with one another. Imagine what would happen if some of the lost individuals from one whale started to join other whale colonies. What if they transmitted the knowledge of how to get rid of human beings?"

For a moment, we thought about our own extinction, and the end of our three-thousand-year history in this world. But Mum was much more optimistic. If they were *that* smart, she said, they would've realized that humans weren't merely simple pests but rather sentient creatures that could be communicated with. They would have tried to talk to us, wouldn't they, instead of just getting rid of us and forgetting about it? Having intelligent company is a good thing, isn't it?

To me, all of this speculation seemed like little more than idle chitchat. Our only real hope was to come across a whale where people were already living, but the chances of that were low. And even if we did somehow find such a whale, the people living on it would be unlikely to take us in now: red heat rash was slowly spreading across our skin, which suggested we somehow had been infected by that last whale. Not that it was the disease that worried us: the prospect of scorching or freezing still terrified us far more.

A week later, we came across something that gave us a feeling of hope.

This was little different from what we'd expected: it was an enormous iceberg. The surface area above the water was huge, about ten times bigger than a normal whale, and we climbed up onto it without even thinking it over too much. Thankfully, a small meltwater stream provided us with a relatively comfortable way to reach the top. We found a giant freshwater lake up there, for which we were grateful, since our freshwater distillation unit had finally started to fail a couple of days earlier.

Icebergs this big weren't uncommon. Warm water currents flowing from Day collided with Night, shearing away vast masses of ice. This iceberg was riding a current toward Day. Maybe not soon, but eventually, it was fated to melt away into nothing. Still, it was a nice to have a little extra time. We could at least fashion ourselves some paddles and ropes using materials taken from the ocean trees that had clumped around the iceberg.

A week passed that way, and then two, and all through that time, the red sun repeatedly appeared above and disappeared below the horizon. It felt like some evil god who controlled our fate was toying with us, giving us a little hope and then a little fear in turn. It was the same with the heat rash spots that disappeared after leaving their marks upon our skin. Was this death or survival? We couldn't know. We heard weird voices before we fell asleep—were they a sign of our brains being infected or just the ghosts that haunted us?

On the day that marked the middle of a month on the iceberg, I found the machine. It was a metallic cylinder, its interior stuffed with complicated devices. What they were for, I couldn't begin to guess. I brought the thing to the doctor, who was filling a water can nearby. The doctor didn't know any better than I did what the device might be, but after we searched around a little more, we found more objects: gloves, pickaxes, and bags of brown chunks that looked like they might once have been food. Finally, we found a single dead body imprisoned inside the ice. The corpse was a man's, beardless and a great deal bigger than us.

"That's our ancestor," said the doctor.

We were looking at the very genesis of our history on this planet.

We considered the opportunity that had been given to us. What else might be inside this iceberg? What if the entire spaceship that our ancestor had ridden here on was still buried somewhere down in this ice? What if the thinking machine inside that spaceship hadn't died yet? What if that machine could save us from this hellish world and send us to some other place?

I howled loudly and sat down. Neither my body nor my brain could handle the overwhelming vastness of this hope that now filled my head. Even knowing that most hope is in vain, and even knowing that we might die leaving corpses steamed in boiling water and covered with red spots, we still couldn't stop clinging to hope. That is why I am writing this now, with a pen and paper that I found buried in the ice. I'm sitting here on top of an iceberg that is slowly melting away, eating a brown chunk of nutriment that I myself yanked from the frost, and as I write this I cling to the hope that this story isn't done yet. I've already salvaged enough paper to write down seven times more than what I've already written so far. Even now, I can't get used to this kind of luxury, being able to use all the paper I want, no matter how much.

What I'm writing isn't the end of this story. So, dear future readers who're obviously reading this, please turn to the next page. A fabulous adventure, completely incompatible with everything I've written so far, surely awaits you there.

Originally published in Korean in
Pandemic, Moonji Publishing Company, 2020.

ABOUT THE AUTHOR

Djuna is a novelist and film critic, and a former chair of the Korean Science Fiction Writers Union. For more than twenty years they have published as a faceless writer, refusing to reveal personal details regarding age, gender, or legal name. Widely considered to be one of South Korea's most important science fiction writers, Djuna has published ten short-story collections and five novels.

The Five Remembrances, According to STE-319

R. L. MEZA

I am of the nature to grow old.

Metal parts that survived fire and shrapnel are no match for the saltwater rushing through the gaps in my armor, spilling between gears and wires, tainting my battered shell with the inexorable creep of rust. Corrosion is a ruthless god. The waves surge inland to drink the mortal corpses littering the shore. The ocean embraces the empty husks, rolling them out to the depths to fill and be filled. I long to sink with them beyond the reach of light's prying fingers. To hear and see nothing while curious creatures explore my insides. To become a home instead of a weapon. But I remain anchored below the tide line, limbs pinned beneath the crumbled monastery wall. Trapped.

The General evaluates my condition with disinterest. When asked if I should be salvaged, he shakes his head. The STEs—or the Salt-The-Earths—are deployed first for a reason: we are outdated. Once activated, we destroy everything in our path, leaving nothing behind. With the red light atop my cranium still burning like a warning, the General delivers his verdict from afar. My targeting system remains active. My free arm clings to a machine gun longer than a man, loaded with lead ammunition. The newer robots have lasers. Their programming allows them to distinguish between worthless meat and valuable targets. They know how to hold hostages and when to take prisoners. They are expensive, held back for crucial operations.

My kind are fodder for the grinder. I was retrieved from an overstocked warehouse, dusted off, greased, and made battle-ready. My fate is a relief to the men who built me. Because I was felled on foreign soil, I'm no longer their responsibility. Demolition and recycling are more costly than building new models. And so, I'll remain here while the army I fought for abandons me. While time marches on, dragging me in its wake. *There is no way to escape growing old.*

I am of the nature to have ill health.

Wind scours my optical sensors with sand. Massive chunks of driftwood cast ashore by raging storms dent my armor and fracture my solar panels. The smoke on the horizon is a constant presence—a nagging, choking reminder of the action that left me behind. I am detritus, half-buried in rock, splattered with bird guano. An assemblage of parts without purpose. My free arm remains cocked at a right angle, gun held high to preserve my sole possession from the hungry tide. My weapon is all that I have, all that I am. I must protect it at all costs.

Relentless waves wear me down. The rubber seals protecting my internal workings crack, then fail. The saltwater invades, devoid of mercy, drowning electronics, bathing my processors in brine. As a cascade of malfunctions tear through my system, I swim in the only madness my kind is capable of: I fire my weapon into sand and sky, babbling to myself in ones and zeros. Active in fits in starts, I lose all sense of time. Men come and go, searching for something. They scour the surrounding cliffs but avoid the beach while the red light burns bright atop my cranium. Without solar, I'm forced to rely on battery power for survival. But, like human life, my battery is finite. Running down. *There is no way to escape having ill health.*

I am of the nature to die.

A fog-blurred figure scampers toward me across the strip of stony gray beach. My targeting system struggles to fix on the shadow darting rabbit-quick over driftwood and rock, scaling the mountain of debris holding me prisoner. I swing my cocked arm around, and the figure freezes. She cowers in the baleful red glow, eyes shiny black with fear—an immature human, nine years past her production date. She possesses the key features condemned by the army that set my kind loose on her people.

She is alone, like me. Vulnerable.

Power sputters in the weak light of morning. The machine gun droops in my grasp. I receive no commands from the computers composing my brain. For the first time in my long life, I don't know what to do. The red light dims.

Panting from exertion, the girl casts a frightened glance over her shoulder. Distant silhouettes bristling with the hard lines of weaponry approach through the fog: hunters. The men who've been searching the cliffs for weeks have finally rousted their quarry from her hiding place. She must be valuable to warrant a search party of two dozen soldiers. Royalty, perhaps. The girl is filthy and gaunt. Her robes are tattered. She must have been starving—desperate—to flee into the open like this.

Something inside me stirs: a spark.

I'm pinned from the waist down, but the maintenance hatch set in my chest is still accessible—or, it would be, if I had a free hand to open it. The spark ignites a strange idea in my cranium. The red light burns like Mars at midnight, like the god of war for which the planet was named. As the barrel of my most prized possession swings outward, I unload the last of my ammunition into the fog to buy time for my final act. Muffled shouts recede toward the cliffs. The girl stares up at me in awe.

Relinquishing the gun is difficult, but the act of loosening my digital manipulators is nothing compared to what comes next. My battery is nearing critical depletion. After several clumsy attempts, I twist the wheel to unlock the maintenance hatch. I hook and pull at the useless parts clogging my chest, casting the wreckage into the waves. I cannot carry the girl to safety, but I can give her a place to hide. I will become a refuge.

The girl stands aside, watching. Solemn. The red light dims then goes dark as I carve out space within my cranium. My final act is to close the hatch behind her after she climbs through my armor. The tide is rising. Water sloshes around her waist, then her ankles, as she wriggles through the neck port into my compact metal skull.

The voices of men grow louder. When they are not greeted by machine gun fire, the soldiers focus their search on the mountain of rubble. They have only a few short hours before the water surging inland severs my husk from the main island, creating a smaller island offshore. The soldiers wrench the maintenance hatch open.

Saltwater churns in my submerged chest. *Nothing could survive in there*, the smallest soldier insists, but he is sent inside regardless. Holding his breath, he bumps blindly against my interior. He misses the neck port and surfaces, sputtering. The man should not be blamed for his oversight; he is a solider, not a technician or an engineer. He is a hunting dog who has lost the scent, left to pace the shore in confusion. The girl, his prize, is curled behind the red light gone dark, floating like an embryo. Face upturned, she harvests tiny sips of air from the silver bubble hovering at the peak of my cranium.

The soldiers retreat. My machine gun vanishes beneath the waves. My battery cools. The spark winks out, extinguished. *There is no way to escape death.*

All that I hold dear and everyone I love is of the nature to change.

The sand buries my machine gun, but not my carapace. The girl survives. Between high tides, she clears the sand from my interior. As her sole companion, I listen to the stories she tells. I learn she is the last of her line—the daughter of a king defeated—destined to become a healer. She fashions glittering lures from the pieces of me that wash up on the beach. She learns to catch seagulls and fish. She feeds herself, growing stronger by the day. Beneath the sparkling night sky, she dreams aloud of a nation reborn from the ashes. She fantasizes about resurrection. Peace.

The soldiers return only once and are driven off by superstition and terror. A rumor circulates among the invaders, of a red-lit specter—a giant—guarding the beach, prone to charge and dismantle with gutting precision. Some call it a god, others a demon. As the rumor spreads, so does the god's territory. Soon, the entire coastline is taboo. Madness invades the army entrenched on the island. The men writhe, sweat-slicked, ranting as if caught in an unending nightmare. Scientists blame the mosquitoes, the air and water tainted by chemical warfare. They dismiss the possibility of a ghostly protector. Disease proliferates; the plundered island is no longer worth inhabiting. The army selects a new target elsewhere, a landmass with fewer mosquitoes and no red lights.

Shadows lengthen and shorten as the seasons pass, as the girl becomes a woman. The woman is no longer afraid. She is strong and resilient. A diamond flecked with salt and sand, she dazzles the eye. She offers the promise of hope, sheltered within her the way I once shielded her from capture. Her smile radiates light like a beacon.

Survivors flock to her, drifting through the monastery ruins like sketches of their former selves. She hears their experiences and heals their wounds. She rebuilds them, one by one. Under her hands, between her fingers, they regain substance, solidifying into a semblance of the people they once were: artists, farmers, herders, and craftsmen. The past tense dwindles from their vocabulary, replaced by the present and, eventually, the future.

Then, the woman leaves me. She packs enough supplies for everyone and leads her followers over the cliffs. Their voices fade, scattered by the wind. *There is no way to escape being separated from them.*

My actions are my only true belongings.

I treasure the memory of a girl seeking refuge inside me. By sacrificing myself to save her, I made a choice independent of programming—my first and my last—an act of free will. Some might call it a malfunction, but I call it a miracle.

For a time, I was a protector instead of a destroyer. I was a home.

And I will be again. The woman has returned, bringing all of the island's survivors with her. The bent and broken populate the ruins. They begin the long process of rebuilding themselves and their monastery, their future. Every morning, they drift toward me through the fog and gather along the shore to offer their thanks. Eyes closed, they empty their minds to exist in the present. To appreciate each moment as if it were their last.

Once a year, on the date when the girl fled the cliffs to float inside my cranium, the woman and her people—my people—build boats of plaster and paper and driftwood. They light candles and set them afloat as the flames burn red.

I cannot escape the consequences of my actions.

My people expand outward from the beach and over the cliffs, channeling life into the territories beyond. Led by a healer, they become a nation once more. The murmur of meditation quiets the memory of explosions. They breathe without fear, slow and deep. Peaceful.

And as their numbers swell, they begin to salvage my remains from the waves. They drag me ashore in pieces. They give me a new shape, a new purpose. They give me a home.

My actions are the ground on which I stand.

ABOUT THE AUTHOR

R. L. Meza is the author of *Our Love Will Devour Us,* published by Dark Matter INK. She writes horror and dark science fiction, and her short stories have appeared in *Nightmare, Dark Matter Magazine,* and *The Dread Machine.* Meza lives in a century-old Victorian house on the coast of northern California, with her husband and the collection of strange animals they call family.

Upgrade Day
RJ TAYLOR

Today is upgrade day and Gabriel, a model 2098 post-human intelligence robotic service assistant, wears an appropriately festive hat. The perfect cone of polka-dotted purple paper slopes to one side of his head, his glossy plastic surface giving the weak elastic band no purchase.

At ten years old, Lilli has a professional approach to birthdays, and as soon as she notices the hat's downward trajectory, she climbs Gabriel's legs and stands tiptoe on his lap so she can straighten it. He smiles. More accurately, the white line of light on his face screen curves upward. But he still thinks of it as a smile. Lilli wraps her arms around him, and he returns the hug.

Juan and Kira, the parents of his family, have been exhibiting signs of anxiety most of the day and now, seeing Lilli embracing him, they trade another glance. These expressions are abnormal. Gabriel considers the data but draws no conclusions. Juan returns to fiddling with the family light tablet, pulling out its extension and aiming its screen at Gabriel.

"Gather for the photo, everyone! Gather!" Juan says and waves to the scattering of other children and family friends sitting throughout the small living room. Lilli sits down on Gabriel's lap and the other young humans pile around them. The older humans are slower to join, but eventually the tablet begins a countdown. Gabriel can't decide if his smile should be five hundred or a thousand pixels wide. He goes for the bigger one first, but then thinks it's excessive and switches back just as the photograph is taken. In the print pulled from the tablet his face screen is a blurred jumble of outputs.

Before he can feel self-conscious, the young humans begin playing with him, and he turns his primary focus toward their entertainment. His secondary processes scan the room for information, curious still about Juan and Kira's anxieties.

"I can't believe you do all this for a machine," an older man says to Kira. He faces away from Gabriel's visual inputs, but the voice matches a business partner of hers.

Kira swallows a little of her drink. "He's a good support for Lilli." She hesitates, then adds. "And he . . . used to be a person."

The man expels a small cough-like laugh. "Used to. Used to. Don't get too attached to your gadgets, that's not healthy."

Kira is silent for only a heartbeat, but Gabriel can read irritation in her features. "He needs to get upgraded anyway."

"And you make it fun for Lilli," the man says, but then his voice drops even lower. "I understand there's some price gouging going on."

"I . . . we made it work this year."

"Next year are you finally switching over? I'm really liking my Rayn—got a JX last summer. More machine than man and much faster processing."

Kira makes a noise, the half-hum Gabriel recognizes as a lack of interest. But the man continues and tells her about his new service assistant for twenty-seven minutes, during which Gabriel tells stories to the children, observes continued heightened tension levels in Juan, and adjusts the climate settings of the room to account for its increased capacity. The party continues, and until the last guest leaves, Gabriel performs his duties with ease, while part of his processing still contemplates the anxiety of his family.

Lilli falls asleep on his lap, and he carries her to her bed. When he returns to the living room, Juan and Kira are standing side by side, a wrapped present in Juan's hands. Gabriel knows it is an upgrade packet, new hardware components for those which will have corroded over the year, easily snapped into place while he runs through system updates.

Other people brought their machines to a service shop only after their systems started malfunctioning, dumped them off and had them shipped back. More still just bought the next model. But Juan and Kira ordered every year's upgrade to be sent to the house just so they could wrap it up for him. "It's not an upgrade day without presents!" Kira said the first year.

"Thank you," Gabriel says now, taking the package, wishing he could express more with his face screen and his voice. Ten years in a robotic body and those desires have begun to fade, but sometimes he misses things. Smell, he misses that most often: baking molasses muffins, fresh cut cilantro, a bowl of lemon zest. And touch. As he tears open the present, he pretends he can really feel the thickness of the paper on his fingers, the silky ribbon falling away, the gloss of the upgrade package.

Except the black box he holds isn't an upgrade package; it's too small, too streamlined. He turns it over and examines it. It's only a software update.

Before Gabriel can express confusion, Juan averts his eyes and apologizes twice. Kira speaks quickly. "We couldn't afford it this year, Gabriel. I know it's disappointing, but . . . maybe next year . . . " She shakes her head. "I won't lie. No, they'll just raise the price again. You have to understand." Her voice is pleading, ashamed. "It's more than we earn in a year."

Gabriel holds the small box in his hand like a baby bird. He cycles through thoughts and emotions, focusing all his powers on finding the reply that will diminish the pain his family feels. "You have treated me so well. I couldn't have asked for a better afterlife."

Kira's lip quivers, and Juan covers his face.

Trying again, Gabriel says, "The update is perfect, I love it."

"It isn't perfect, Gabi," Kira says, voice thick, "But it's all we have."

"Might as well enjoy it, then," Gabriel says, trying to keep his tone light and all the crushing catastrophic thoughts at bay.

He sits down and they hook in the update package, and then Kira kisses his head, and Juan gives him a hug.

A second before he falls into the trance of the update, he asks, "Does Lilli know?"

Juan shakes his head. "Not yet."

Gabriel gives a tiny nod and then succumbs to the loading screen.

He had expected much, much worse when he'd died.

He had sold his afterlife to a robotics company, living freely off their salary until the very moment of his death when his brain became theirs. Then they poured his neural network into a servant assistant frame, and he became a slave to whomever purchased him. He had the right education, genetics, and aptitudes to appeal to the company, but when the day had come to sign the contract, he had hesitated.

He had seen pohos, post-hominid intelligences, before and noticed they brought out a particular type of malice in their owners. They seemed compelled to assert dominance over the former humans, calling them only by their model number, using them as furniture or otherwise humiliating them. Aside from being cheaper and easier to acquire, the preformed networks of a human mind had also become more consumer-palatable than the generated intelligences involved in the AI incidents of the sixties. Fear of those incidents and the new anxiety that, in theory, anyone could become one, made those who were never actually in danger of falling so far need to separate themselves from the machines, to establish a clear line between human and post-human. Between people and things.

Gabriel wanted to be a chef, though, to cook the most delicious food the world had ever tasted. He wanted to invent dishes, to name them, so a hundred years later across the world someone would order a Lemon Gabriel and a trivia-obsessed friend of theirs would point out that the fluffy mess of deliciousness they were about to consume was actually named after someone named Gabriel. And that future-person would roll their eyes at their friend and dig in with abandon.

After he'd gone through culinary school, he'd had six-digit debt and watched as his friends worked until two in the morning every night, just trying to stay afloat, having a hit or a drink to ease the total exhaustion. He didn't want his life to look like that. If that meant selling his afterlife, well then. He thought of Faust as he signed the contract screen and pressed his eye against the retinal scan.

But when he checked his bank account the next day, he fell to the scratched floorboards of his apartment, crying. Some part of him hadn't believed it was real. He cried that entire day, tears of utter relief.

And he had gone on to invent dishes, had created a small restaurant that lost money every year, but was adored by the locals. Maybe he would have created the Lemon Gabriel, and maybe it would have been enjoyed a hundred years later by someone on the other side of the world and their annoying friend. Maybe. Except that on his twenty-eighth birthday as he was leaving his restaurant to head home for the night, a truck running on virus-riddled software jumped the curb and ended his life.

He consoles himself in his servitude with three things. First, he was able to live the life he wanted. Second, the family that owns him is kind. And third, he never had to grow old. But now, as he rises back into full awareness from the updates, he realizes he will age. His hardware, his body, will begin to corrupt, and eventually even the updates will fail to keep his software running properly.

Kira stands in the doorway watching him. He pushes his pixels up into a smile. She will watch him die, as will Juan and Lilli. Poor Lilli. One of his first duties had been tending to her infant needs. Now she will watch him slowly corrode. An eccentric quadrillionaire who'd chosen a robotic afterlife might manage to pay for a mind transfer to a new body when their model began to fail. Death, they joke, is the new puberty. But a service assistant is single-use, and as his model becomes obsolete, so does whatever remains of his mind.

Kira pulls a stool over and sits beside him. "Updates done?"

He unplugs. "Done. Thank you."

"Juan and I talked last night, and we came up with an idea." She examines the screen of his face. "Do you, Gabriel, think you made the right choice, back," she waves vaguely, "back there?"

When a poho service assistant is created, it keeps its human memories and emotions even as it is filled with new programs, such as a compulsion to obey commands and a damper on personal ambition. As an extra safety measure, pohos are assembled as far away from their former human lives as possible, starting them in a fresh new afterlife. "I made a good life," Gabriel replies, "back there. It's over now." He thinks he ought to feel sorrow—he never became famous, after all—but feels instead gratitude. He had expected true slavery to be the cost of pursuing his dreams.

Kira nods. "I think . . . I am going to apply."

It takes Gabriel a few moments of processing to understand. "No!" The outburst of emotion is more than his auditory output can convey.

Kira is taken aback. He hardly ever raises his outputs. "But . . . then . . . " she stammers, "we could pay for your upgrades."

Gabriel tries to form his thousand thoughts into a coherent sentence. "I was lucky. I am lucky." No. That isn't quite what he wants to say. "Don't destroy tomorrow for today. Not for me, not for this." He waves at his robotics, the whole of him.

Kira leans back, eyes wide. "But . . . Lilli."

"If I were a dog, you'd have me put down."

"Gabriel! You're a person."

"Then let me face it. Like a person." He puts a hand gently on her knee. "Let me accept what I am."

Her lip begins trembling again, but she nods.

And so Gabriel lives, as much as a machine can. His processes slow, lag. After a few years, his hardware begins to malfunction. He holds on. He holds on until Lilli is out of school. In the photograph of her graduation, he is in the back, stuck in a seated position, shuddering and shaking, most of his motor functions shot. But he wears a thousand-pixel smile.

Not long after, his core processes fail. His face screen flickers for a day and then goes black, and all the tiny electrical impulses of a lifetime, or two, dissipate for the last time.

ABOUT THE AUTHOR

RJ Taylor is a queer speculative fiction writer based outside Boston whose work explores themes of escape, transformation, and non-human consciousness. She's a member of the Codex writer's group and a recent graduate of Viable Paradise. Her short fiction has appeared in *Factor Four* and *Apex Magazine,* and is forthcoming in *The Magazine of Fantasy & Science Fiction.*

Beyond the Godzilla Trope: Radiation Biology
JULIE NOVÁKOVÁ

We all know the story: a radioactive spider bites you, and the next thing you know, you're shooting webbing out of your . . . wrists? Or you accidentally lock yourself in a test chamber and end up at first disintegrated, then becoming a godlike superhero. In another instance, radiation turns a prehistoric lizard into a raging Godzilla.

These tropes are as old as pulp science fiction itself, but they are far removed from the reality of how radiation affects our bodies. Here on Earth, we are under normal circumstances mostly protected from harmful radiation, but that's not the case if we travel outside the confines of our planet's magnetic field. When we return to the Moon, as planned for the near future, and embark further into our solar system, we'll need to find ways to protect ourselves and all the life we take with us. If we don't, we can't expect to turn into superhumans; rather, we could expect cancer, cognitive disorders, infection . . . How serious is the cosmic radiation threat, really, and how do we avoid the gravest scenarios?

Caught in a Solar Storm

What exactly happens if a human or animal body receives a high dose of radiation? The first thing is, there is no one-size-fits-all answer. What happens would depend on the type of radiation, the time frame, and the means of exposure. There is a whole zoo of what we call radiation: electromagnetic radiation, like gamma rays, x-rays, and UV radiation, and multiple very different kinds of particle radiation. The particles in question can have vastly different speed, mass, charge (or none), and while some can be stopped by as meager protection as a sheet of paper and some are thwarted by a little aluminum, against other ones we would need thick layers of heavy materials. Heavy, of course, is a problem in space travel, where every extra kilogram is felt dearly in the amount of fuel needed for acceleration or deceleration.

On Earth, we tend to be worried about UV radiation: we put on sunscreen, try to limit our exposure to direct sunlight ... UV is relatively easy to block. Besides, the protective effect of Earth's ozone layer, windows, mineral or chemical filters in sunscreen, and some fabrics can protect us from most of it. In space, it would be blocked by the hull of the ship, walls of a base, or a space suit. We would mostly need to worry about various kinds of particle radiation. The Sun constantly emits particles we call solar wind: mostly accelerated protons with some alpha particles (helium nuclei) and a few heavier ions. Sometimes, though, it can release enormous amounts of energy at once.

The alternate history series *For All Mankind*, episode "Every Little Thing," tried to showcase the dangers of getting caught in a solar storm. A solar flare can propel a huge mass of charged particles, called a coronal mass ejection (CME), into space. If it hits the Earth, it can destroy satellites, interfere with radio communication, and in the case of an extremely strong flare, even do some damage to electronics on the planet's surface despite the protection offered by Earth's magnetic field and atmosphere. On the Moon, astronauts would have no such protection. They would have to seek as much shelter within their base as possible, or, in case of being caught on a mission outside, shelter in a lava tube, as shown in that episode.

In *For All Mankind*, the astronaut caught outside in a solar storm eventually suffered loss of eyesight. In reality, we could expect many vastly different outcomes based on the intensity of the CME, length of exposure, and individual variation. Most of what we know about the effects of radiation on the human body is based on the lives of survivors of atomic bomb explosions and nuclear disasters, to a lesser extent on epidemiological studies of populations from places with high natural radiation background, hard-to-generalize case studies of isolated criticality accidents, and abhorrent Cold War human experiments from both sides of the Iron Curtain.

An atomic bomb blast releases gamma rays and x-rays as well as particle radiation: neutrons, electrons, and alpha particles. In a nuclear disaster such as Chernobyl, many different radioactive isotopes of various elements escaped into the environment, releasing different types of radiation with a speed based on their half-lives. Either is difficult to compare with cosmic radiation sources, not just because of the different types of radiation, but also because survivors inhaled and sometimes ingested radioactive compounds, which resulted in more severe damage to their lungs and gastrointestinal tract. Cosmic radiation doesn't present this risk, but it includes (as a minor constituent in comparison to protons or alpha particles) accelerated heavy nuclei, something we rarely encounter on Earth.

Although each kind of radiation requires different protection and has somewhat different effects on the body, the general principle remains the same: radiation ionizes many of the molecules it hits, causing them to become chemically unstable and starting harmful chemical reactions, or "just" damaging them so that they don't work anymore. If enough damage to the DNA accumulates, it can't always be repaired in time, and the cell will eventually die. If that happens to enough cells, failure of whole tissues and organs can ensue. That's the gist—and that's why radiation poisoning is so dangerous. Only *extremely* large doses would kill a person immediately or within minutes, hours. But a lethal or near-lethal dose badly damages sensitive tissues, such as the bone marrow or gastrointestinal lining, resulting in the depletion of white blood cells and heightened risk of succumbing to infections. To a lesser degree, they would be at risk of depletion of red blood cells and anemia. In cases involving gut diarrhea, they could experience disrupted nutrient intake, water and electrolyte imbalance, and eventually death. Internal bleeding can also occur. Death can take days or weeks—but after receiving lethal doses, it's difficult to prevent even with medical interventions like blood transfusions, bone marrow transplants, and IVs delivering nutrients and carefully selected antibiotics to the body. If we imagine ourselves on the Moon, shielded just by our space suits and unable to take cover in time, how likely is it that this horrific fate would await us?

Luckily, it's not very likely even in the case of a strong CME. The amount of radiation received by a person can be measured in Roentgen Equivalent Man, or rem. An x-ray at the hospital gives you roughly one rem; nothing you should worry about. On the Moon, protected only by your space suit during a solar storm, you would probably receive between a few dozen and a hundred rem, in the worst-case scenario a few hundred (the actual value would depend on the size of the CME and whether the most intense flow of charged particles would hit you directly). A few dozen rem is not nearly enough to directly kill you, but it would cause sickness and dramatically increase your likelihood of having cancer in the coming years. A few hundred could be fatal. The estimated fatal dose, if received at once, is approximately three hundred rem. Receiving immediate intense medical care, most people would still survive this in the short term but developing cancer would be practically a certainty rather than a likelihood, and they would probably suffer from a variety of other problems, including an impaired immune system, anemia, cataracts, cognitive issues, or seizures. These long-term effects can vary wildly, even if we consider the same type of radiation and same dose received. Studies of long-term effects, such as the incidence of different types of cancer, come mainly from the survivors of Hiroshima and Nagasaki blasts as well as the Chernobyl disaster, and they are still ongoing. It appears that age and sex play a role, but there can be huge individual variation—something to be aware of when sending people to space.

Space Radiation Exposure: Death by a Thousand Cuts?

In space, we can expect some sudden events, such as the CMEs, and need to be prepared for them. What interplanetary travel mostly amounts to is constant exposure to somewhat higher-than-healthy doses of radiation—something for which it is more difficult to find analogs for on Earth. To some extent, we can turn to epidemiological studies of people living in radiation-polluted areas, such as the vicinity of the Techa River in South Urals, or high natural background radiation locations like India's Kerala or Iran's Ramsar. The trouble is, these places tend to have low populations, and we still need to separate the effects of radiation from age, sex, environmental, and cultural conditions. For instance, if we look at lung cancer, we need to find out how many local people smoke and how much, whether there is non-radiation industrial pollution . . . Such studies need very thoroughly and carefully collected data, appropriate statistical methods, and large enough sample sizes—and it's not always possible to have it all. That's why we still don't know how health effects the radiation scale. Does the damage increase linearly with the dose, or does it follow a more complicated pattern? Some researchers think that very low doses—barely surpassing the usual natural background levels—are actually beneficial to cells, triggering protective mechanisms that help us repair damage not just from radiation. It also depends on if you ask radiation scientists who are "more statisticians," "more physicists," "more physicians," or "more biologists." Answering this question reliably is not just relevant for spaceflight; attuning the dose and timing of cancer radiotherapy is no easy feat, even though such therapeutic doses cannot be considered small.

If we want to study radiation's effects on life in more controlled conditions before we venture "out there," we must turn to experiments on other species. The trouble is, most such studies used only one specific kind of radiation, like accelerated neutrons, iron particles, carbon ions. It's not easy to realistically mimic the composition of the solar wind, and especially cosmic rays, so studies typically use a limited range of particles and their speeds. It's also more difficult to find studies of prolonged, even multigenerational, exposure (let me know if you happen to find a rat colony living inside a particle accelerator). In multiple animal species, radiation exposure appeared to be linked to memory and cognitive deficits, disrupted thermoregulation, and other problems, but it's mainly short-term or one-shot studies, some with whole-body exposure and some using only irradiation of the head or spine, not always specifying the test animals' ages, and usually delivering higher doses than can be realistically expected during spaceflight, making it hard to generalize besides "radiation may be bad for your cognition." A rare chronic exposure study on mice, using space-relevant doses, showed that memory and recognition were impaired, and the animals exhibited more social avoidance and anxiety (not something you'd want in a spaceship crew!). The damage can be quite varied and lasting beyond the exposure time. Combined with radiation-induced immune deficits and other problems, it could be a dangerous mix for space travel.

Is there a way to connect this to actual astronauts' health? Astronauts who stay long in space tend to suffer from a variety of health changes and issues: impaired eyesight and immune system, DNA damage, buildup of fluids in the upper body, and muscle atrophy. While some are clearly effects of microgravity, other changes probably result from several factors, and radiation could be a contributing factor, if perhaps small, because astronauts on the ISS are well within the Earth's magnetic field and are protected from most charged particles from the Sun or other cosmic sources. During a round trip to Mars, they would probably receive about sixty-six rem, give or take, barring events like strong CMEs. That is well below a lethal dose, not speaking of the fact that it wouldn't be received at once, but over the course of approximately two years. But it's nothing to simply shrug off, either. No space agency wants to condemn astronauts to substantially increased risks of cancer, neurological problems, and other health issues in the years to come. The expected Mars voyage dose surpasses NASA's whole-career exposure limits (although there is an ongoing debate about whether—and how—these should be changed).

Humans are very sensitive to radiation, but not all life shares this trait. There are many microbes, but also some multicellular organisms, that are extremely resistant to most forms of radiation. Could we, perhaps, borrow biotechnological solutions from them in the future?

"Microscopic Godzillas"

The world of microbes continues to yield surprises in terms of what conditions the bacteria, archaea, or various protists in question can survive, or even thrive, in. Radiation resistance is no exception. Some microbes live quite happily in nuclear reactors or waste sites. The bacterium *Deinococcus radiodurans*, thriving in nuclear reactor coolant tanks (though in that, it's not alone), is the most famous example. It can readily survive at least three orders of magnitude more radiation than a human, and it's uniquely capable of reassembling and repairing broken DNA strands, while the manganous ions it contains may also help. Archaea have their champions too: *Thermococcus gammatolerans*, discovered in deep-sea hot hydrothermal vents, has been shown to survive four orders of magnitude more radiation than it would take to kill a human.

Still, *Deinococcus* and *Thermococcus* are prokaryotes. Our last common ancestor lived some *four billion years* ago. Can we find a radiation-resistant organism closer to us? We can look to tardigrades, also famous can-take-it-all survivors, whose common ancestor with us lived in the Ediacaran, some six hundred million years ago. These little critters, distant cousins of arthropods, usually live in wet moss or lichen or aquatic environments and eat microbes, plant fragments, or each other. These unassuming microscopic animals are famous for being able to survive many kinds of adverse conditions, even their combinations, and that includes radiation (although *veryextreme* doses appear to make them sterile) and direct exposure to space. They can become dormant and desiccated quite quickly, resuming activity and repairing damage once conditions return to normal. How can they survive several orders of magnitude more radiation exposure than most other animals, though? The answer may lay partly in a special protein dubbed Dsup, as in damage suppressor, which appears to act as a scaffold supporting DNA and preventing breaks. This tardigrade protein greatly increased the survival of cultured human cells irradiated by strong x-rays.

It's not just tardigrades among multicellular organisms, though; bdelloid rotifers, some flies, crustaceans, nematodes, cockroaches . . .

But it's much harder to find radiation-resistant vertebrates, much less mammals. Rodents appear to be slightly more radiation-tolerant than humans, but nowhere near easily surviving the highest recorded doses survived by people. Could mammals use some of the mechanisms of, for instance, tardigrades to survive greater doses? So far, such biotechnological applications remain in the realm of science fiction—but for how long?

Future space exploration brings forth many challenges, and radiation is certainly one of the most pressing. What would best help assess the risks are studies right in the cosmic environment; it doesn't get more realistic than that. So, when you hear about plans to keep tardigrades, insects, or rodents in future lunar bases, think of the many open questions they could help us answer.

ABOUT THE AUTHOR

Julie Nováková is a scientist, educator and award-winning Czech author, editor and translator of science fiction, fantasy and detective stories. She published seven novels, one anthology, one story collection and over thirty short pieces in Czech. Her work in English appeared in *Clarkesworld, Asimov's, Analog,* and elsewhere. Her works have been translated into eight languages so far, and she translates Czech stories into English (in *Tor.com, Strange Horizons, F&SF, Clarkesworld,* and *Welkin Magazine*). She edited or co-edited an anthology of Czech speculative fiction in translation, *Dreams From Beyond,* a book of European SF in Filipino translation, *Haka,* an outreach ebook of astrobiological SF, *Strangest of All,* and its more ambitious follow-up print and ebook anthology *Life Beyond Us* (Laksa Media, upcoming in late 2022). Julie's newest book is a story collection titled *The Ship Whisperer* (Arbiter Press, 2020). She is a recipient of the European fandom's Encouragement Award and multiple Czech genre awards. She's active in science outreach, education and nonfiction writing, and co-leads the outreach group of the European Astrobiology Institute. She's a member of the XPRIZE Sci-fi Advisory Council.

Violent Revolutions:
A Conversation with S.L. Huang

ARLEY SORG

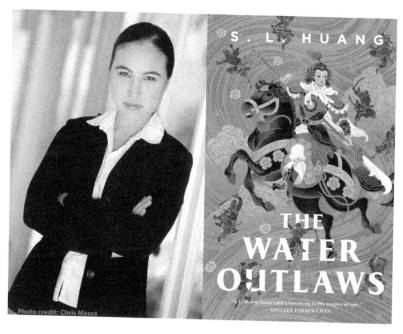

Photo credit: Chris Massa

S.L. Huang grew up in New Jersey and has since lived in many differ-ent states and four different countries, more recently ending up near Chicago. Huang did undergraduate research in computer sciences, then carried this focus over into taking many courses at MIT, while majoring in math. Huang also minored in theater arts. "I also would have had enough for a Chinese minor if they hadn't canceled the last classes I needed, but I did go and teach computer science in China, so that was a win."

For eight years so far, S.L. Huang's primary occupation (in terms of time commitment and income) has been writing. Huang also does tech consulting (primarily in machine learning and natural language processing) and works as a stunt performer and weapons expert in the film industry. "There's an article on Wikipedia somewhere that lists me as a world-famous swordmaster. This is not remotely true, but I find it hilarious and have never corrected it. I am very good at swords, though. That's what I took workshops in during college instead of writing."

In 2014, S.L. Huang self-published a novel, *Zero Sum Game*, which was followed closely by the Book Smugglers' publication of *Hunting Monsters*. Online magazine *Strange Horizons* published short story "By Degrees and Dilatory Time" in 2015, and Book Smugglers released *Monsters* follow-up *Fighting Demons* not long after.

Over the next few years, Huang's work appeared in many notable venues, such as *Daily Science Fiction*, *Analog Science Fiction and Fact*, and *Nature*, leading up to the Tor Books release of *Zero Sum Game* in 2018. The following year, Tor Books published sequel *Null Set*; Serial Box published several installments in the Vela serial, which were written by Huang; and Tor.com published short story "As the Last I May Know," which went on to win a Hugo Award. Tordotcom Publishing released novella *Burning Roses* in 2020, while Tor Books released *Zero Sum Game* and *Null Set* follow up *Critical Point*. Huang's novelette "Murder by Pixel: Crime and Responsibility in the Digital Darkness" came out in the December 2022 *Clarkesworld* and was an Ignyte, Nebula, and Hugo awards finalist.

S.L. Huang's latest book is Tordotcom Publishing novel *The Water Outlaws*, just released in August.

Your latest book, The Water Outlaws, draws inspiration from 水滸傳 *(Water Margin) by* 施耐庵 *(Shi Nai'an), perhaps also by* 羅貫中 *(Luo Guanzhong), and maybe others. What was your approach or intention in terms of the relationship between that book and your work?*

Oh, I love *Water Margin* so much.

I've long been a strong fan of remix culture. I believe we're always in conversation with everything else. My pieces that aren't explicitly retellings are doing that, too, just less obviously.

It's worth mentioning that when reimagining a book like *Water Margin* that is so culturally significant, I feel like there are always questions of fidelity and authenticity that come into play. I love *Water Margin*, but I'm not a *Water Margin* scholar. I'm also not a Chinese person from China; I grew up in the United States. There's a nervousness that comes with that, cultural questions of "rights" and "authority."

I poured so much research, respect, and joy into this reimagining. My editor, Ruoxi Chen, is also a lifelong fan of *Water Margin* and brought her own cultural understanding to the table, which was unspeakably wonderful, and Tor was kind enough to hire a cultural consultant who *is* legitimately a scholar in *Water Margin* (who was GREAT!!) to make sure I wasn't doing anything I didn't mean to.

But as far as what I did mean to do—well, I knew going in that I was never going to retell this the same way a person who grew up in China would retell it. I'm also not going to retell it the same way a man would retell it, or a straight person, or someone who wasn't interested in the questions I'm interested in, the things that speak to me about the original book. I decided I had to lean into that. For instance, I didn't try to stamp out all of my influences from the Western epic fantasy I grew up on; instead, I tried to be conscious about my choices with those influences.

Those of us with several heritages, or who are from immigrant families—there can be a lot of hesitancy and anxiety about connecting with our ancestral cultures. But there's something very, very ugly about the idea that migration removes our right to do so, especially when so much of migration might not be people's first choice but instead happens under involuntary or dangerous circumstances. I deeply and passionately reject any idea that this means we can't or shouldn't forge our own relationship with culture, with our own perspectives, ones that might be different or complicated but that equally deserve to be out in the world.

And a property like *Water Margin,* which has been retold and reclaimed and reimagined in a thousand different ways over centuries—I like to think it has room for all of us to show our own love of it. I know there will still be people who question whether I had the "right" to gender-spin it or write an adaptation in English or what have you, but to them I just say . . . I join the very strong tradition of *Jin Ping Mei!*

(*Jin Ping Mei* is, as some might know, a *Water Margin* "fanfic" that was written a few hundred years later and is now itself an extremely famous novel and a classic of Chinese literature in its own right. It is also famous for having seventy-two on-page kinky sex scenes to *Water Margin's* zero.)

To me, *Water Margin's* cultural history is all about creative interpretations, from the very beginning!

What drew you to Water Margin in particular, what was it about this work that spoke to you, or that made you want to cast certain aspects of it in a different way?

Well. It's *fun*.

Seriously, you might hear the words "classic Chinese novel" and think of something dry and boring. *Water Margin* is AMAZING. It's packed with action and sword fights and antiheroes and absurdity and dirty language. It's not what most people probably imagine for classic literature!

Of course, it's also very . . . male. There are one hundred and eight bandits, and one hundred and five of them are men. (Surprisingly, there are three female bandits, all of whom are great characters, and at least one of them—Hu Sanniang—is clearly depicted as being able to best most of the men. I've kept her female in my gender-spun version.)

The misogyny in the whole book is pretty rough. Women mostly only show up to be adulterers or victims, or, occasionally, to commit a heroically pure suicide. The one saving grace, which frankly keeps the book as readable as it is, is that there's a surprising lack of sexual violence—it's occasionally implied, including in one place I did incorporate for my novel, but *Water Margin* likes to keep it oblique.

So, yeah, the obvious solution in my version was to gender-spin it. In my view of feminist and queer history, it is not strange at all to find a large group of women and/or queer people in a patriarchal society— instead, it is very natural. We always find each other! My bandits became a self-selecting group who choose each other *because* of who they are; their unusual roles and identities are not random but are part of *why*: part of why *this* group of bandits, part of why they feel so keenly the injustice and corruption of the Empire.

Are there specific advantages and challenges to drawing inspiration from a specific text, and to placing a story in a specific historic time frame?

Oh, absolutely. I dealt with it by doing the approximate equivalent research to a master's thesis. It *still* never felt like enough . . .

Did the book change in any significant ways from initial concept to final product, over drafts, edits, and so on?

Like all books I've written, the form of it did change quite a lot as I drafted, and I figured out how to bring it together, but nothing of remarkable significance—it pretty well-matches the proposal I first sent to Tor!

The Water Outlaws *is concerned with the tyranny and oppression that existed in a specific time and place. Are there important ways in which this book also speaks to issues of our present day and place?*

Oh, absolutely, of course.

I spend a lot of time these days thinking about the concept of revolution, and about governmental power. In liberal spaces, which is the majority of my social groups, there's sometimes a measure of . . . glibness, I suppose, about revolution in contexts of criticism of the government.

What worries me—what *frightens* me—is that violent revolutions very rarely seem to go right, across history. A lot of people die. A lot of the most vulnerable people die. My own family fled a violent revolution because *they* would have died. We see this over and over again, people rising up—often justly, against tyranny!—but then people with that same corruption and hunger for power take over from within the revolutionaries, and too often bring an even worse oppression than before.

This feels real to me because my family lived it; because I grew up on stories of it. It's never felt academic.

And, simultaneously, I am as angry as everyone else at what we see some powerful people daring to do to their fellow humans in 2023. Like many, I desperately want to push back against it, to make a difference in fighting it.

Add to that: I'm in several minority demographics. There have always been a lot of demands on us. To be beyond reproach, so "they" have no excuse. To be loud, because being quiet is complicity. To be less angry; to be more angry. To prove ourselves this way or that way instead of just being able to live. And one thing I think people in the majority often don't see is how *complicated* that can get, not only for each individual, but intra-community, among those of us might make divergent calculations on things that are deeply important to all of us. We often say that demographics aren't monolithic—there are so many strands of humanity, of response, of choices . . . especially in reaction to these sorts of pressures and demands from society.

And sometimes, when put in hard places, we're capable of making bad decisions. Sometimes it's understandable. Sometimes it's because there are no good decisions. Sometimes it's impossible to *tell* what the good decision is.

This doesn't sound-bite well. But I spend a lot of time, a lot a *lot* of time and brain cycles, thinking about things like power. About the ways we respond to injustice, and how *understandable* so much of it is . . . whether it's being "too quiet" *or* "too angry" . . . or "too" whatever else someone else might test and make demands for . . .

And then, separate from that, what the costs or consequences of that understandable thing might be.

The bandits in the original *Water Margin* are some of the OG antiheroic Robin Hoods, stealing from the rich and giving to . . . well, mostly themselves, but *sometimes* the poor. Incredibly engaging, even endearing! And I'm far from the only one to think so, but they're not "nice." Song Jiang murders his wife in cold blood, quite brutally. Li Kui and Wu Yong are fan favorites, but the hotheaded Li Kui has a memorable scene in which he *kills a four-year-old child* in order to force the hand of someone they want to recruit. *And he does it on Wu Yong's order.* There's lots of fighting against unambiguously evil and corrupt government officials, to be sure, and many of the bandits have suffered mightily at the hands of Imperial oppression. But there's also plenty of filling their own pockets and deciding "stab first, ask questions later."

They're nominally our heroes—but mostly because the novel tells us so, repeatedly.

I truly do love their epic, ridiculous, incredible story. But that dichotomy plays into so much of what bounces around in my own brain regarding power and injustice and violence.

I wanted to write bandits who did horrible things in extremely understandable ways. Bandits who include both people who are fighting for what's right and people who are fighting to grasp for their own selfish goals—and sometimes they're the same people. I wanted to write rage and dishonesty and power struggles and self-preservation, and also idealism and loyalty and friendship and justice, and survival and humor and compromises, and have it all make *sense* that people are doing these things, because that feels real to me.

You might be waiting for a conclusion here, a "therefore this is how we ought to react to injustice in our world." I don't really have one. I didn't write *The Water Outlaws* to take a stance—unless it is the very simplistic one of "tyranny bad," which I think we can all agree on! Among my bandits, I wanted to explore our *reactions* to tyranny. I think—I hope—that every one of them is understandable, even at their most horrifying or frightening decisions; and I hope readers will still root them on among their joys and triumphs.

Finally—it means something, I think, to put the ambiguous morals of *Water Margin* into the additional context of people who are the targets of a misogynistic and repressive patriarchy. In my version, Song Jiang is a woman, and she has a backstory of having killed her husband—in a reflection of the original Song Jiang killing his wife. When my Song Jiang is asked why she did it, she tells us:

"For all the reasons husbands so frequently need killing. But the law does not recognize a wife's rights here, alas."

It's no doubt exactly the same sentiment the original Song Jiang might have had about *his* spousal murder. That it was perfectly righteous, just peskily illegal. Yet, I love that line because I feel like it reads so very loaded, now that I've switched the genders.

I don't endorse murder, generally. But I also want people to read that from my Song Jiang and feel a heavy suspicion that they'd still be on her side.

What are your favorite things about the main character of *The Water Outlaws*, Lin Chong, and what were the most challenging or satisfying things about writing her?

I mentioned above that I wanted to show people's different decisions and reactions to oppression and patriarchy. Lin Chong starts out the book as the extreme example of *keep your head down*. She both challenges society by existing in the position she has, and simultaneously refuses to challenge it at all . . . at least not until she's forced to.

One of the other characters has basically the opposite journey.

I said above that I wanted to write people who all make different calculations and have them all be sympathetic, even if those choices are heartbreaking. Those two crossing character arcs were absolutely planned in from the beginning. The model minority who realizes she has to stand up and fight . . . and the opinionated activist who discovers that in reality, it's not as easy to make these judgment calls as she assumed from the comfort of distance.

I don't judge either of them for how they choose at the beginning. Nor at the end.

There's one other thing I loved about writing Lin Chong, and that's that she's a teacher. And it's *important* that she's a teacher, and that she's a *good* teacher; it's not just incidental.

It's a bit subtle, but it informs every part of her plot and character arc. She's important politically because she's a teacher. The bandits want her because they want her skills at instruction; she won't just bring her own fighting skills but can broaden *theirs*. Her own journey with the supernatural, and with learning, is in conversation with her whole teaching identity.

Pedagogy absolutely fascinates me, and I think is highly underrated in its power. Lin Chong's power isn't only that she's a fighter, but that she's a *teacher of fighting*, and I love that.

In the publicity run-up for this book, I thought about writing an article about protagonists who are teachers. Not side characters—not wise mentors who often die; there are *plenty* of those—but the main protagonist being a teacher, and where the teaching part is important. Only . . . I couldn't think of any.

I asked around. And hardly anyone else could think of any either! So I had to drop the idea.

Who are some of your favorite characters, besides Lin Chong, and what do you like most about them?

Ohhh, this is hard because I like all of them, but I guess I would say Lu Da and Wu Yong.

Lu Da is most readers' favorite so far, partly because she's *funny*, good-hearted, and bold and unselfconscious. She's really a delight.

Wu Yong—who is my sister's favorite, and admittedly one of mine too—was delicious to write partly because of . . . well, I somewhat whimsically call Wu Yong my brilliant darling sociopath. Not quite true, as there's definitely a fanatical loyalty to the bandits mixed up in there, along with an especial loyalty and love for Song Jiang.

But Wu Yong is *exactly* the type of character who does all the wrong things for the right reasons. Or, sometimes, the right things for the wrong reasons. Ingenious, arrogant, ruthless, and furiously moral (for some blue-and-orange values of moral)—that's Wu Yong.

What were your goals in terms of the use of magic or the fantastic in this book?

I very consciously chose a somewhat subtler approach, like what I see in a lot of Chinese media—where it's organically part of the world but not necessarily the core focus of the worldbuilding. I'll be interested to see what people in the West think!

Additionally—this wasn't part of the *Water Margin* reimagining, but in addition to the part that's a retelling, there's a subplot of the book that is basically my love letter to Song Dynasty history. The Song Dynasty had an absolute *explosion* of technology and innovation. After all, this is the era and the people who invented gunpowder, paper, the printing press, paper money, and the compass (all of which make an appearance!). So I took great joy in adding a plotline that's basically the characters "sciencing the magic."

After all, if magic were an accepted, almost mundane part of your world . . . wouldn't you? How would you even know it was "magic" that caused ghosts and somehow something totally different and non-magical that made the sun rise or the seasons change?

The Locus Magazine review of The Water Outlaws calls it "gloriously cinematic." In terms of craft, what is the key to delivering a cinematic narrative?

Heck if I know! I feel like I should be able to say something much smarter about this. It's mostly just vibes, to be quite honest!

I *am* quite chuffed at that quote, though. It's exactly what I was going for.

What is the heart of this story for you, what is most important about it, beyond blurbs and reviews?

That it's FUN.

Sometimes—especially for culturally connected work—I feel like we're driven to write something "important," that "says something." Although I do hope I've done justice to the themes talked about here, I primarily want *The Water Outlaws* to be a joyous, page-turning adventure.

After all, we're not going to have true equality until *everyone* can write the fun books!

What else are you working on, what do you have coming up that folks should know about?

The Water Outlaws is definitely what's eating my month right now!

Next book news is still under wraps, but lately I've also been doing a lot of game writing—for something completely different that has *no violence at all*, I have a contemporary cozy baking show game up on Storyloom. It's interactive fiction where you're a geeky engineer who enters a baking competition!

Tina Connolly and I are also almost done serializing a shared-world comedic fantasy game that's an absurdist fairy tale remix, in which Red Riding Hood is best friends with the Wolf, Rapunzel turned her hair into snakes (she was sick of people TOUCHING IT), and Jack is a con artist and thief with socialist leanings and a hobby in magic bean hydroponics. It's fun and funny and queer and full of feels (and Tina is HILARIOUS and amazing!).

Tina's half is here, with the wonderfully dysfunctional and somewhat violent royal princesses. And I've got the scrappy woodlanders! (Likewise dysfunctional and somewhat violent. But good hearts.) We designed them so that they *can* be read separately, but they're definitely better together; I recommend starting with Tina's and then switching back and forth every quest.

Finally, folks might know that I'm up for the Hugo right now, in two categories. Right here in *Clarkesworld* is "Murder By Pixel: Crime and Responsibility in the Digital Darkness"—which is also up for the Ignyte Award!—and is about machine learning and harassment and the choices we make with technology. I wrote it a full year before ChatGPT came out, but they debuted on almost the same day. It's been dizzying seeing the world news catch up with the story; when I wrote it, it was a *very* niche idea.

I'm also up in Best Related Work for my nonfiction article on writing pedagogy. *That* was a very deep rabbit hole. I spent months and months across so many sources writing it, but as I said above . . . pedagogy is both fascinating and very serious to me. Especially when the CIA is involved.

I've been humbled and amazed at what a big impact the article's had on how people think about teaching (or learning) creative writing in SFF, and I'm currently part of other efforts to help build new models for our writing and workshopping classrooms.

ABOUT THE AUTHOR

Arley Sorg is an associate agent at kt literary. He is a two-time World Fantasy Award Finalist and a two-time Locus Award Finalist for his work as co-Editor-in-Chief at *Fantasy Magazine*. Arley is also a SFWA Solstice Award Recipient, a Space Cowboy Award Recipient, and a finalist for two Ignyte Awards. Arley is senior editor at *Locus*, associate editor at both *Lightspeed* & *Nightmare*, a columnist for *The Magazine of Fantasy and Science Fiction* and an interviewer for *Clarkesworld*. He is a guest critiquer for the 2023 Odyssey Workshop, and is the week five instructor for the 2023 6-week Clarion West Workshop, among other teaching and speaking engagements.

Global Discovery:
A Conversation with Jared Shurin
ARLEY SORG

Jared Shurin was born in Kansas City and moved to London in his mid-twenties. He wrote his high school term paper on William Gibson's *Neuromancer*, he is a BBQ judge, and he lives with three cats, who "fit the meme perfectly: one thinks she's a person, one thinks he's better than a person, and one doesn't think about anything at all." He worked in communications for roughly twenty years, starting with advertising, "everything from sneakers to oven cleaner." Over the recent decade his focus has been supporting the public sector, charities, and NGOs, helping them to use communications to support "tackling challenging and complex problems, ranging from climate change to creating opportunities for young people." Prior to these, Shurin had a range of posts, from weekend shifts at Barnes & Noble to fortune-telling to bartending private parties. "Like everyone else, I've worked in food service. I'm deeply suspicious of anyone that hasn't."

The *Pornokitsch* site began in 2008 and was run by Anne C. Perry and Shurin. The site showcased features and reviews "written by a rotating team of regular contributors," including Becky Chambers, Kuzhali Manickavel, Mahvesh Murad, Molly Tanzer, and others. They founded a notable set of awards called The Kitschies in 2009, "with the purpose of rewarding intelligent, progressive, and entertaining fiction."

Shurin's anthology editing journey began not long after. "My wife and I saw that there was an upcoming exhibition at Tate Britain, featuring the apocalyptic paintings of John Martin. The apocalypse was *the* SFF trend at that point, and we were shocked to see there was no corresponding book. We ran a big review site at the time and were very full of ourselves. We pitched the idea to publisher contacts, who all wisely pointed out that the exhibition begins in three months, which is, in industry terms, 'basically tomorrow.' Being complete idiots, we thought to prove them all wrong and went for it ourselves. Thus began a pretty good run as Jurassic London." Beginning with *Pandemonium: Stories of the Apocalypse* in 2011 (edited by Perry and Shurin)—which featured authors such as Lauren Beukes, Jonathan Oliver, Andy Remic, and others—Jurassic London produced over forty books and gave all the profits to charity.

Pornokitsch itself was well-regarded. It was a finalist for a 2011 British Science Fiction Association Award for Non-Fiction, a 2013 British Fantasy Award winner for Non-Fiction, a 2014 Hugo Award finalist for Best Fanzine, and a finalist for the r/fantasy Stabby in 2016. "We were even selected for *The Guardian*'s h.club100 as 'innovators and pioneers in the creative industries,' which sounds very glamorous."

Some of the Jurassic London titles saw similar recognition: *A Town Called Pandemonium* (Perry and Shurin) was a BFA finalist, *Speculative Fiction 2012* (Justin Landon and Shurin) was a Hugo finalist and a BFA winner, and *The Book of the Dead* (Shurin) was a Shirley Jackson finalist. In 2017, Rebellion imprint Solaris published anthology *The Djinn Falls in Love & Other Stories*, edited by Shurin and Mahvesh Murad, which was a finalist for Locus, Shirley Jackson, and World Fantasy awards. Murad and Shurin followed this up with *The Outcast Hours* (Solaris, 2019), which was also a World Fantasy Award finalist. Shurin also edited two installments of *Best British Fantasy* for NewCon Press.

Jared Shurin's latest anthology is due later this month from Penguin Random House imprint Vintage, called *The Big Book of Cyberpunk*, "over a hundred stories from more than twenty-five countries that both establish and subvert the classic cyberpunk tropes and aesthetic—from gritty, near-future noir to pulse-pounding action."

You've been editing anthologies for over a decade now. Has the role of anthologies in genre changed over the years?

There's probably a good argument that starts with "now, more than ever . . . " but, honestly, we've always needed mechanisms for discovery, and we always will. Anthologies have always played a role in creating, curating, and promoting stories; often giving them a new lease on life and helping them connect with more readers. They're a fantastic way for readers to encounter new voices, rediscover classics, and see new perspectives on a theme.

My own introduction to, and education in, science fiction and fantasy (well, beyond Dragonlance and Lone Wolf) came from anthologies. Boxes and boxes of them, bought at library sales and flea markets. Lots of old books with names like *Best of the Hugo Almosts, Volume 27*, and *Asimov Presents Knight Presents Blish Presents More Asimov*; or enticing names like *Spaceswords!* or *Demons from that Planet that's Right Behind You.*

What has changed about your own approach to putting together anthologies?

Confidence, really. I've now been doing this for over a dozen years, both on my own and with a variety of (truly wonderful) partners. Editing an anthology, whether that's commissioning originals or collecting reprints, is a series of choices. What's the theme, what's the brief, who do you want, how will you find them, what do you want to bring out in a story, what kind of story do you want . . . all the way down to the order of the table of contents.

In the early days, I was so delighted just to "be in the room," that I let a lot of those choices be made for me or traveled the path of least resistance. When I think about some of the first anthologies—there are some fabulous stories in there, but are they always fabulous *anthologies*? Is there the special editorial *something-something* that lifts this book into being more than the sum of its parts? I think that challenge is particularly critical when it comes to reprint anthologies. Are you collecting or are you curating? What are you, the editor, adding to this work?

I'm being a little hard on myself: I love every book I've ever been involved with and am proud of them all. But when I look at the great editors, they have a very distinct voice. Take Ann VanderMeer: you're not buying a collection of stories on a theme, you're buying *her* unique perspective on that theme. Her voice comes from the confidence to make hard, consistent choices, resulting in powerful, interesting work. In the immortal words of Liz Lemon, "I want to go to there."

Your latest anthology is The Big Book of Cyberpunk. Is it important to distinguish cyberpunk as distinctive from science fiction in general? And in what contexts might it be important?

One of the overlooked twists of cyberpunk's origin story is that it arose more from postmodern literature than it did science fiction. That's hugely important. The "punk" in cyberpunk is about pushing back against The Man and The System, and it is *also* a rebellion against the modes, traditions, and forms of how stories are told. Early cyberpunk isn't about revolution, it *was* the revolution; gonzo, disruptive, noisy literature that, in and of itself, was a form of fighting back against convention.

This angry, humanist mode of storytelling captured how people felt about the pace of change prompted by technological advance. Cyberpunk, with its nontraditional narratives, disillusioned protagonists, multifaceted societies, and oblique conflicts, was a natural way of capturing that twitchy, unsettling relationship that we had with the future we were promised.

Now, to a certain extent, all genre labels are bollocks, and it would be exceedingly *un*-cyberpunk to throw up exclusive barriers. But for practical purposes, there is a difference between cyberpunk and science fiction. Part of this distinction stems from the genre's non-SFnal parentage; the rest from its continued commitment to those roots. There's always a new windmill to tilt at, problem to be examined, or axiom to undermine. Science fiction, ultimately, is about unfettered possibilities. We absolutely need that in our fiction and our lives. Cyberpunk examines the fetters; literature that grounds wonder in our humanity.

Are there kinds of science fiction that are often erroneously called "cyberpunk," but which are, more properly, something else?

I think it helps to think of cyberpunk as two different genres: the thematic and the aesthetic. For the most part, I generally default to talking about "thematic" cyberpunk. It comes in a range of shapes and sizes, but, however it looks—whatever tropes it contains or world it inhabits—it tackles the themes of cyberpunk.

It so happens that a couple of the seminal works of cyberpunk, stories that really sparked the imagination and went "mainstream"— *Neuromancer* and *Blade Runner*—also shared a particular aesthetic. Neon, rain, urban settings, chunky decks built on 1980s technology. Curvaceous androids with mirrorshades. The look and feel of these important stories were so appealing, so inviting, that it spawned its own creative movement. People wanted to play in, visit, and—most importantly—write this world.

Thematic purists are disappointed by aesthetic cyberpunk's lack of robust message. But those attracted by the aesthetic don't recognize "real," thematic stories as cyberpunk. Is one interpretation correct? Cyberpunk is contemptuous of the shallow and populist—but it is equally disdainful of snobbery.

There's no question to me that the aesthetic is the more well-known of the two interpretations. The compelling *vibe* of cyberpunk has continued to recruit new generations of fans. To ring-fence some sort of "trucyberpunk" would be a betrayal to those who have been busily flying the neon flag.

I've tried to pull together a book that encompasses *all* of the genre. It doesn't so much bridge the divide as cross-sell it and show that cyberpunk can be cyberpunk even if it is—or isn't—neon. *The Big Book* is firmly rooted in the themes, but that doesn't mean I turned my nose up at stories with fast cars, big guns, and sexy robots. I'm a big fan of all three in my fiction. I mean, just look at the cover! I don't personally believe that neon and rain *make* something "cyberpunk," but nor do they exclude it from being so.

The stories in this book span nearly seventy-five years, the most recent selections published in 2022. What are some of the most important changes you see in cyberpunk fiction throughout this period?

Early cyberpunk was a sausage-fest. You can't really put lipstick on that pig. It was a lot of dudes, writing dudily. That's not to say women weren't involved or significant. Pat Cadigan was (and is) writing some of the best cyberpunk fiction, Ellen Datlow commissioned virtually every OG cyberpunk work for *Omni*, and legendary figures like Donna Haraway were publishing "A Cyborg Manifesto," using the metaphor of technology to challenge existing assumptions of gender in society.

But, like broader speculative—and nonspeculative—literature at the time . . . early cyberpunk was a sausage-fest.

If there's one thing to say in cyberpunk's favor, it is that it didn't take *long* to sort itself out, and I think the very nature of the genre led to people jousting against systemic inequalities in gender, race, and class. Cyberpunk is a genre about challenging conventions and was quick to—rightfully—call itself out. Take Candas Jane Dorsey's "(Learning About) Machine Sex," for example, which is a scathing response to patriarchal tech culture. The genre has kept interrogating itself and pushing forward, and I think this positive change applies (if slightly less successfully) to issues of race and class as well. As a result, the modern contributions in this book are vastly more inclusive—across every dimension and definition—than the older stories.

There are also two areas where cyberpunk has, legitimately, led the way since its early days. Cyberpunk has been a global genre since its inception. I suspect this is indirectly—if not directly—because the genre is a response to globalism; on top of responding to more "micro" societal challenges that are shared across all contexts, and not unique to a specific, Western, context. *The Big Book* has contributors from over twenty countries. That includes first translations of truly classic cyberpunk stories, such as Victor Pelevin's "The Yuletide Cyberpunk Yarn, or Christmas_Eve-117.DIR" and Gerardo Horacio Porcayo's "Ripped Images, Rusty Dreams." There are plenty of modern stories in there from around the world, but it was important to me to demonstrate that *global* cyberpunk isn't a recent phenomenon.

The other area where cyberpunk is exceptional is in its diversity of publication. Cyberpunk has always pushed the definition of "publishing"—with stories appearing not only in books and magazines, but zines, textbooks, pamphlets, liner notes, and early hypertext documents. This is just as true now: great cyberpunk stories may first appear on websites, on social media, serialized or self-published; in a variety of fascinating forms. It made seeking out stories for this book *incredibly annoying*. On one hand, you could be eating a hamburger and find a cyberpunk story on the wrapper. On the other hand, you have to spend hours on eBay battling for a waterlogged copy of an old game manual, in the hopes that the micro-fiction inside is worth reprinting (reader: it was not).

What is the relationship between cyberpunk fiction and visual media like television and film, or even games, like video games and the iconic Shadowrun role-playing game from 1989?

I'm a book guy, so I'm always going to say "the book did it better," but that's not *really* true. (Has anyone actually *read* the original *Godfather*? It is *terrible*.) Cyberpunk, of all genres, shouldn't—and can't—turn up its nose at other forms of media.

Let's be honest: *Shadowrun* got more people interested than all zines combined, and *Fortnite*'s cyberpunk season has given the genre another generational lease on life. It would be equally impossible to conceive of a cyberpunk without *Blade Runner*, *Max Headroom*, *Akira*, *The Long Tomorrow*, *Cyberpunk 2077*, or *The ArchAndroid*.

Every form of media brings something different to the party. What I love about cyberpunk is that it has always been open about wandering across the bridges from one to the other. That's how you get Jeff Noon writing "Ghost Codes" created as a combination of tweets (RIP) and liner notes, or Janelle Monáe and Alaya Dawn Johnson writing a novella inspired by Monáe's album.

Cyberpunk is also a form of fiction that openly plays with, and responds to, popular culture. In *The Big Book*, you have Omar Robert Hamilton responding to Britney Spears, Cassandra Khaw examining diet culture, Isabel Fall reclaiming a toxic meme, and Lavie Tidhar doing something very strange with celebrities. Cyberpunk is predicated on the fact that soft media deserves the same level of literary scrutiny as hard science; that arcade games are as worthy of meaningful fiction as FTL drives and the atomic bomb.

Looking at the table of contents and the copyright notes, The Big Book of Cyberpunk draws from a fantastic range of sources, including both the expected (such as Clarkesworld and Asimov's) to the unexpected (such as Mississippi Review) to the obscure. What was your process for sourcing titles and making selections?

That 1987 issue of the *Mississippi Review* is like the cyberpunk Dead Sea Scrolls. Larry McCaffery (speaking of legendary editors) brought his critical clout to assembling and examining the genre and turned the proto-genre into a credible literary movement. It was later expanded into the anthology *Storming the Reality Studio*, which, alongside *Mirrorshades* and *Semiotext(e)*, is probably the most significant and *defining* assemblage of cyberpunk literary voices.

Assembling the book was such a daunting task that my normal, slightly haphazard, approach wasn't going to work. I began with the (few, but very good) existing survey anthologies and the (many, and of variable quality) academic works. I compiled a seed bibliography, and it snowballed from there. I gleefully read the complete run of *Omni*. And *Mondo 2000*. And *The Infinite Matrix* and *Flurb* and … I plowed through decades' worth of *Wired* and *Nature*. I scrounged many, *many* piles of zines, clicked a lot of creaky old websites, asked for recommendations in a lot of—very different—online and offline places, and generally made an ass of myself snooping around the cyberpunk world. A *lot* of anthologies were involved, as you might expect. My seed bibliography has now bloomed into over one thousand items. I am become death, the destroyer of book recommendation threads.

For a supposedly short-lived and self-contained genre, there were a lot of paths to go haring down. Worse(?), as a genre initiated by technically savvy people, a lot of materials are still available and extant (if poorly cataloged). The hamburger wrapper scenario never actually happened but wasn't outside the realm of possibility. And if said wrapper ever existed, there are probably grainy .bmp files of it in a thread somewhere. *Files I need to find.*

I'm happy to say that even the more whimsical approaches paid off: I found Michael Moss and his excellent story by asking for suggestions on Reddit, for example. For that matter, I was introduced to Erica Satifka by literally typing "cyberpunk" into Amazon. Perhaps the most unexpected legacy of this book is the first time, ever, someone successfully using Amazon for "discovery."

Selections are organized into sections within the book, such as "Self" and "Culture." Are there organizational principles at work behind the order of appearance of stories within these sections?

The Big Book of Cyberpunk, is in fact, a *really,* big book. At one thousand one hundred pages, double-columned; over a hundred stories, and nigh on seven hundred thousand words. That's about six or seven "normal" anthologies. That's a lot of material to play with.

What I wanted to show was the *importance* of cyberpunk; how it is (and was and will be) relevant to many of the key discussions that we're having across many facets of life. What does cyberpunk fiction say about how technology impacts our sense of identity? How does it comment on our consumption of, and by, culture? How does cyberpunk explore how technology has changed our relationships—friendly, professional, familial, or adversarial—with one another? What about technology's impact on our ability to change and challenge the system we live in?

I drew on Marshall McLuhan's prophetic concept of a "global village," a world intimately connected by media and technology to inform these key questions. Within each of these anthology-length sections, the stories run from a cyberpunk "precursor" through "classic" cyberpunk stories, and up to, as much as possible, the present day.

I'm not going to lie—it is a deeply self-indulgent way to organize an anthology. But it was a lot of fun to put together, and I hope just as much fun to read as well.

Are there stories here that may particularly surprise some readers, and how so?

I don't want to spoil anyone. It is a naturally surprising genre.

You mentioned *Shadowrun* earlier, and there are two stories from that universe in here. Possibly the first "tie-in" fiction in *The Big Book* series? But, as we discussed above, you couldn't have modern cyberpunk without it.

And one story that, in and of itself, is surprising from start to finish: Minister Faust's absolutely madcap "Somatosensory Cortex Dog Mess You Up Big Time, You Sick Sack of S**t" is exactly as provocative and hilarious as the title sounds. A cozy, family-friendly take on billionaire entitlement that will warm the cockles of your heart.

What are a few of the stories that stand out most for you or were especially important to you, and why?

I've mentioned a few of the translated pieces already, another is Bef's "Wonderama," which is also appearing here for the first time in English. It weaves together some classic cyberpunk tropes—most notably a virtual world—and has something quite sinister to say about the power of nostalgia. The ending gives me shivers.

Sunny Moraine's "I Tell Thee All, I Can No More" is horrifying. And beautiful. And then you think about it again, and realize it is really, *really* horrifying, but you also can't unsee how beautiful it is. It is the drone romance we deserve.

Vauhini Vara's "Ghosts" was the first piece that I had slotted into the table of contents. I knew from the start that it had to be the final story in the anthology. It captures everything about our troubling relationship with modernity: our continuous need for answers, our dependence on technology, our need for significance in the face of chaos and noise.

Are there a few pieces here that you feel deserve more recognition than they received?

George Alec Effinger is often left off the list of cyberpunk giants, and that's a shame. The Marîd Audran series is phenomenal cyberpunk. The worldbuilding of the Budayeen is brilliant, the characters are fantastically layered, the whole thing is genuinely progressive, and—shock of shocks—it is a piece of science fiction "noir" that is, genuinely, noir. *When Gravity Fails* (1987) is a lost cyberpunk classic, and I'm glad for the chance to reprint one of Marîd's shorter adventures in here.

I also feel that Justina Robson's contributions to the genre are overlooked. "The Girl Hero's Mirror Says He's Not the One" is a compact cyberpunk thriller, complete with action, weird tech, and an identity crisis. When it comes to fusing the themes and aesthetics of cyberpunk, this one is right at the center—it would look great under neon lights but also hits you like a train.

In your editor's note, you briefly but frankly discuss the fact that some of the older pieces are problematic. In a world that is rich in fiction, what is the value of reading decades-old fiction with problematic elements?

The value of reading these stories is that they're pushing back against the unjust and unfair systems of their time. Some of the stories are problematic, but that's by intent: the cyberpunks were trying to create problems. When the stories are offensive or transgressive, it is because the authors were using objectionable means to highlight the cruelty or absurdity they perceived in the systems around them. It is a genre that is provocative and provokes, and it *definitely* crosses some lines.

That said—there are moments where the stories are unintentionally offensive as well. These are stories that come from different eras, with different norms and standards in what language was acceptable. I can only hope those elements don't distract from the story's overall message and its cultural significance as part of a movement. These stories and authors were (and still are) fighting the good fight.

As we discussed waaaay back at the start: we live in a world where we have more choice of what to read than *any other moment in human history.* It is kind of amazing! And, because of that, *it is absolutely OK to not read things*; for any reason. Transgressive themes and offensive content are all better-than-OK reasons to *not* read things. That's why it was important to me that the note was in there. I wanted people reading this book to be aware of its contents. Deproblematizing cyberpunk was never going to be an option, as the genre itself will always be pushing boundaries. As editor, my role is to make sure my selection shows how the genre is at least trying to push the *right* ones.

Were there pieces that you would have liked to include in this book, but that didn't make it in for some reason?

I have an "unthology" of stories that I couldn't acquire for some reason or another. The rights were in a complicated place, the fee was prohibitive, I couldn't find a way to reach the author or their estate, the author/ agent never responded, or I just botched the deal. Each is a lesson learned, I suppose.

Do you have advice for folks interested in putting together an anthology?

Time, even more than money, can be a huge barrier. You're wrangling twelve, twenty, or one hundred individual works. Don't underestimate the administrative horsepower that you'll need to get through this.

For an anthology of original works, I've found that the hard work isn't in finding contributors but comes in the back and forth of editing the stories. However you try and manage the process, you, yourself, will eventually become the sticking point, with a dozen authors patiently awaiting their edits. That said, helping that creative process is an absolute joy, and nothing beats the feeling of being the very first person to read a new work, written by one of your favorite authors, *just for you*.

For reprint anthologies, like this one—minimal editing! Someone like Ellen Datlow or Neil Clarke already commissioned and edited the story, so all you're doing is stealing valor. The bad news is: you're tracking down the rights holder, haggling the contract, and doing a lot of paperwork. *That* said, the research is so much fun, and you get to spend your time "working" by reading all sorts of strange and esoteric things in search of treasure. And nothing beats the feeling of rediscovery, and the sense of pride that comes from bringing it to new readers.

You've read a lot of fiction over the course of a decade. For you, who are some of the most exciting newer voices in fiction, and who are a few of the authors that you are always eager to read, even after years of reading their work?

I had the honor of judging The Kitschies this past year, so I am currently awash in genre fiction's finest authors (at least, those who published in the UK in the calendar year 2022). W.P. Wiles' *The Last Blade Priest* is an absolutely astounding epic fantasy that hits exactly the right balance of subversion and love. You can't really write a revisionist epic fantasy without really, truly *loving* epic fantasy, and it is clear that Wiles comes from that place of respect, while also pushing into exciting new territory.

Other new, or newer, voices I loved from this year's reading included Emily McGovern's *Twelve Percent Dread* (a graphic novel that captured the essence of being a contemporary Londoner), E. J. Swift's *The Coral Bones* (a time-tangled story about perseverance in the face of catastrophe), Ayanna Lloyd Banwo's *When We Were Birds* (atmospheric and wonderful, with worldbuilding that takes you on the journey), and Julia Armfield's *Our Wives Under the Sea* (how can a story be so good at weird *and* so good at love?).

Erica Satifka, she-who-I-found-through-random-Amazon searches, is my go-to for contemporary cyberpunk and is doing fantastic things. Molly Tanzer, also in this anthology, refuses to be confined to a single genre, which always leaves me curious (and a little nervous) about what she'll do next.

Probably not what you were expecting, but Tessa Bailey is an auto-buy for me, and Katie Shepard's debut, *Bear with Me Now,* is the best contemporary romance I've read in a while. I'm still laughing about the otters.

What else are you working on? What do you have coming up that you'd like readers to know about?

I have two very different anthology proposals sitting in inboxes right now. One is an original, one is a reprint. I'm honestly not sure which path I'll be going down. Exciting times!

ABOUT THE AUTHOR

Arley Sorg is an associate agent at kt literary. He is a two-time World Fantasy Award Finalist and a two-time Locus Award Finalist for his work as co-Editor-in-Chief at *Fantasy Magazine*. Arley is also a SFWA Solstice Award Recipient, a Space Cowboy Award Recipient, and a finalist for two Ignyte Awards. Arley is senior editor at *Locus*, associate editor at both *Lightspeed* & *Nightmare*, a columnist for *The Magazine of Fantasy and Science Fiction* and an interviewer for *Clarkesworld*. He is a guest critiquer for the 2023 Odyssey Workshop, and is the week five instructor for the 2023 6-week Clarion West Workshop, among other teaching and speaking engagements.

Editor's Desk:
A Farewell to Kindle Subscriptions
NEIL CLARKE

Clarkesworld launched in 2006, so we've had a front row seat for how digital publishing has reshaped the genre short fiction market. While a lot of credit is given to online fiction opening up a much wider and global readership, its survival has been almost exclusively due to digital subscriptions and ebook sales.

When the Kindle was unveiled in 2007, ebooks and ereaders had already been around for a while, but still catered to a niche audience. Amazon's entry into the landscape eventually ended up reshaping the field and claiming a sizable market share in the process. They popularized the medium, creating opportunities not only for publishers, but authors as well. It was by no means perfect, but it's hard to argue that it wasn't historic.

Growth in the ebook space came at a pivotal time for the short fiction genre magazines. Online magazines were very small and barely scraping up enough to pay their authors from donations and other sources. Print magazines were bleeding subscriptions and suffering from visibility problems. The whole "short fiction is dead" thing was in full-swing, but the medium was really just wounded.

That would change over the next few years. One of the biggest things to turn that around was the Kindle Newsstand. At the start, the program was invite-only. *Asimov's* and *Analog*, as part of Penny Publications, were the first two science fiction and fantasy magazines to get on the platform and, as such, benefited from the extra visibility and early placement in the program. While print subscriptions still dominated their revenue for a number of years (digital now leads), it brought in many new readers, providing additional financial stability.

While we were able to sell individual ebooks through the Amazon KDP program, the revenue it generated for the magazine fluctuated from month-to-month, making it difficult to budget around. In February of 2011, when we started selling digital subscriptions and ebooks issues through Weightless Books, each issue still contained only two stories. Despite year-after-year increases in readership, we were never able to afford more. Weightless provided some stability, but not enough to build on. This is not a knock. Stability was a gift I will always be grateful for. We love and highly recommend Weightless Books.

Later that year, our application to join Amazon's Kindle Publishing for Periodicals program was accepted and we became the third SF/F magazine available for subscription there. They paid us monthly, on-time, and without fail. The visibility and opportunities by being both on that platform and being an early-adopter benefited us greatly. For the first time in *Clarkesworld*'s history, we moved from stability to growth. We didn't always manage that growth wisely, but it created opportunities to work with more authors, take on bigger projects, and become what we are today.

Amazon subscriptions rapidly became our largest source of revenue. Ever concerned about having all our eggs in one basket, we continued working with Weightless and added Barnes & Noble, Patreon, Clarkes-worldCitizens, and even dedicated apps as they became available to us.

While we've had some success with a few of those, others of those didn't work out. One vendor turned out to be the source of pirated ebooks distributed online. Another stopped paying us, which is why we no longer have Apple and Google apps. Some vendors were simply dismissed due to predatory pricing and others thought we were too small to bother with. Through all of this, our greatest fear was that Amazon would tinker with the royalty rate. Little did we know that we'd have to contend with them shuttering the whole program instead. It's a whole different scale of problem.

This is the last month our Kindle subscribers will receive an issue from us. We'll receive our final payment from Amazon next month. Somewhat begrudgingly, we accepted an offer to have *Clarkesworld* in a new Kindle Unlimited program for magazines. (The terms are different from what they have for books.) This is very much about revenue recovery for us. By agreeing, we will earn about half of what we used to. That could go up or down when the next annual contract comes in. That all depends on how many people READ and spend time on the issues published in Kindle Unlimited.

Just as Amazon opening subscriptions had a significant impact on the field, closing them will be felt by more than just those directly affected. I've called this a "call your parents" moment for short fiction readers. If you love short fiction and the magazines that publish them–whether or not they were in Amazon–make sure you support them by subscribing if you want to see them find stability and the ability to become all they are meant to be.

I warned you earlier this year that I would have to beat this particular drum quite loudly. I apologize for repeating myself, but this is one of those important moments in the history of the magazine. Our future has shifted back into uncertainty and this is the last issue in which I can talk to those subscribers.

There are over *1800* of them. No, we don't know who they are. Amazon doesn't share.

If you are currently subscribed to us on Amazon, we hope this isn't goodbye. If you are already subscribed elsewhere, thank you. If you've never subscribed or lapsed, now would be a really good time to come back. Next month is our seventeenth anniversary issue. With your support, I hope to celebrate many more.

ABOUT THE AUTHOR

Neil Clarke is the editor of *Clarkesworld Magazine, Forever Magazine,* and several anthologies, including the Best Science Fiction of the Year series. He is a ten-time finalist and current winner of the Hugo Award for Best Editor (Short Form), has won the Chesley Award for Best Art Director three times, and received the Kate Wilhelm Solstice Award from SFWA in 2019. His latest anthology, *New Voices in Chinese Science Fiction* (co-edited with Xia Jia and Regina Kanyu Wang), is now available from Clarkesworld Books. He currently lives in NJ with his wife and two sons.

Escape

COVER ART BY IGNACIO BAZAN-LAZCANO

ABOUT THE ARTIST

Ignacio Bazan-Lazcano is a concept artist and currently works as a principal illustrator at Rockstar Games.

Printed in the USA
CPSIA information can be obtained
at www.ICGtesting.com
JSHW020826120923
48146JS00003B/17

9 781642 361476